A Dream of Africa

CAMARA LAYE

A Dream of Africa

translated from the French by JAMES KIRKUP

with an introduction by EMILE SNYDER

COLLIER BOOKS, NEW YORK, NEW YORK

The Macmillan Company
866 Third Avenue, New York, N.Y. 10022

First published in French under the title *Dramouss* by
Librairie Plon, 1966.
First English translation published by Wm. Collins Sons &
Co., Ltd., London, in 1968 and is reprinted by permission.

Library of Congress Catalog Card Number: 70-156991

FIRST COLLIER BOOKS EDITION 1971

Printed in the United States of America

896
L427dxk

Contents

*This book is dedicated
to the young people of Africa*

. . . But especially to the young people of my own
generation and my own Native Land, who, not having
enjoyed the easy successes of their younger brothers,
and separated long years from their parent country,
and dispersed throughout the world in search of more
effective weapons for the fray, have for the most part
returned to that parent country unprovided with the
full armory of modern equipment they had dreamed of
bringing back with them, but their memories crowded
with adventures and their hearts inspired by a certain
emotion—all of which things, that they might bring
benefit to the rising generation, deserved to be related
with sincerity.

. . . As a witness of solidarity and friendship to all, I
make a vow that this story, indited with swift-flashing
quill, shall serve not just as an example, but rather as a
basis for objective criticisms which shall be of profit to
our young people and to the future of our Native
Land. May this work contribute to galvanizing the energies of that youth; and above all to awaken the dy-

namic energies of our young African poets and prose writers who are still seeking each other out, or who, already known to one another, are endeavoring to speak out with a greater, a much greater voice in the long process of the total restoration of our native ways of thinking—those ways of thinking that, in order to resist the ravages of time and temporary fashion, must of necessity draw their essential force from the historical truths of our respective civilizations, and in African realities . . .

. . . I write this book in order that African ways of thinking, re-integrated and restored in this manner, may be a new force—not aggressive, but fruitful.

. . . I desire to liberate that extraordinary power of sympathy that lies deep in the hearts of every one of us; I desire that we should learn to dominate our passions so that this essential sympathy may be encouraged to grow and come forth in every one of us, to make it more active and ever-present among us, to allow it free play so that our message, the message of the authentic African spirit, consciously and resolutely engaged on the path of tutelary wisdom and reason, may spread its seeds among all of us.

. . . It is the author's desire that the incommunicable should be communicated, and the ineffable hearkened unto.

Introduction

THE MAN SITTING across from me, Islamic fashion, legs crossed, his chest a little bent forward—as he has evolved his father in his writings—a man dressed in an unadorned white *boubou*, and living in a modest house in Conakry, teeming with the noise of children (while in independent Guinea it was already the fashion for certain ministers and intellectuals to occupy splendid villas and be driven around town in a black Mercedes-Benz), the man, Camara Laye, observed me with great concentration. His eyes plunged straight into mine, locked with mine in moments of warm intensity, seeking to reveal the thoughts behind their gaze while at the same time trying to gauge my own thoughts. On his lips a latent smile, ready to bloom at the first provocation.

My first recollection of Camara Laye had this immediacy, this authenticity, this direct and warm acceptance as when an African, in French-speaking West Africa, says to a man he likes, *"mon frère,"* my brother. I had just arrived—Christmas 1963—at Conakry from a long truck drive across Upper Guinea, down through the Fouta Jalon to the coast. And as I

described to him my marvelous journey through Sui-
giri, Kankan and Kouroussa—sites of Camara Laye's
childhood—I could feel my friend's mind move back in
time, to that happy childhood he recalled in his first
work, *The Dark Child*, 1953.

For that is what strikes you first about Camara
Laye, the man and the writer: this intense love for his
country, this almost ancestral love he seems to wrap
himself in as he does his body in the white *boubou*.
The opening pages of *A Dream of Africa* are perme-
ated with it. Setting foot in his country after six years
of absence in Paris, Fatoman speaks of the beauty of
Guinea which he constantly personalizes with the pos-
sessive case: "my native land," "my homeland," "my
Lower Guinea." Here there is no empty or arrogant
boast, no traditional patriotism inherited from the absorption of too many governmental slogans, but a personal return from exile into the familiar paths, the
spiritual reknitting with the past which Camara Laye
values and from which he has acquired much of his
wisdom.

Sent to Paris after technical secondary school training in Guinea, Camara Laye first tasted the loneliness
and the coldness of a city he had perhaps overidealized
in his mind, as many young African schoolboys were
bound to do, in former colonial times. Soon after his
arrival, working as a mechanic at the Simca motor
factory, and caught between the impersonal density of
an industrial world and the solitude of a small hotel
room, Camara Laye came to retrace with words, and
for himself alone, the image of his father and mother,
of his friends, of the great Niger River, of the seasons
of harvest, of the ancestral rites of his clan, and re-
assess the permanence of the spiritual values instilled in
him through a strict Koranic upbringing tempered with
the boisterous warmth of an African childhood. And as
he bent his mind over his roots, Camara Laye wrote:

It seems that my mother, my father were living by my side. I was talking to them, they were talking to me. I seemed to be again living in their warmth, my heart was full of their warmth. And above my head, it was not the miserable electric light over my table, and the papers on which I was hastily scribbling, it was the sun of Guinea, the implacable sun of Africa itself, pouring its light over me.

The Dark Child was a personal and lyrical statement. It was received as such by French critics who praised the sensitivity of the young writer, the clarity of his prose, and the felt authenticity of his memories. Yet the autobiography was attacked by a more overtly militant African writer, the Cameroonian Mongo Beti, for its failure to involve the colonial administration in the recovery of the past.

If *The Dark Child* was an autobiography, centered upon a privileged cluster of images, it was nonetheless a projection of a type of African life that was either unknown or scoffed at by the average French reader. At a crucial turning point in the ulcerous history of colonialism, when the French found themselves harassed into making more and more concessions to their colonies, *The Dark Child* offered a corrective image of Africa—the presentation of a cohesive society, structured internally through traditions and moral principles, and for whom the values of communal living, respect for individual personality, a formal code of manners and a deep religious sentiment were basic to its very conception of life. The ethos of *The Dark Child* stood in subtle opposition to the harsh experience of Western society, barely recovered from the horrors of a Second World War, atrocities and the dehumanization of man. *The Dark Child* not only affirmed—in an unpretentious manner—the African's moral values, it indirectly challenged some of the compromised foundations of Western culture.

The universe of *The Dark Child* is a warm, felicitous

universe, that Léopold Sédar Senghor of Senegal calls
the "Kingdom of childhood." But the confidence of
Camara Laye is not born out of naïveté, nor out of
beatitude. He knows that we live in an age of anxiety,
that the balance of wholesome and fecund forces is
constantly threatened by malevolent spirits, be they the
spirits of nature or the anguished spirit of man seized
by a passion to explain everything, to possess the physical universe and yet to retain the privilege of eternal
salvation.

A decade separates the publication of *The Dark
Child* from the writing of *A Dream of Africa*, which
existed in manuscript form as early as 1963 but was
withheld from publication for political reasons. During
this decade Camara Laye's faith in the sustaining value
of the "Kingdom of childhood," and in the basic goodness of man, was put to a hard test. In 1958 refusing,
singlehanded, General de Gaulle's referendum to join
the French Community as an intermediary measure
to complete independence, Guinea proclaimed its own
Guinean Republic. The event marked the initial political involvement of Camara Laye with the Guinean
"Experiment." Called to political life by Sekou Touré,
he occupied diplomatic posts in Liberia and Ghana.
Later he was named Director of the *Centre de Re-
cherche*, in the Ministry of Information. During these
"official" years, Camara Laye came to know the growing labor pains of an independent nation, the subtle
ramifications of power and the corruption of a dream
by opportunistic and unscrupulous politicians. His crit-
ical attitude of the political practices, his soul-search-
ing analysis of ideologies insofar as they applied practically to the betterment of "his" Guinean brothers, led
him to a life of semiretirement. Having refused to
"jump on the bandwagon," he found himself watched
by the political hierarchy suspicious of doubters, of
privateers, of selfless men while all around the fruits of

independence seemed ripe enough for the greedy ones to pluck.

A Dream of Africa is, for its writer, a betrayed dream. Similar expressions of frustration for the aborted promises of independence are found in the novels and poems of African writers in English. In the "urban" novels of Chinua Achebe, in all the Lagos work of Cyprian Ekwensi, and in the poems of Lenrie Peters and G. Awoonor-Williams—to mention only a few—we find the same bitterness toward the African exploiters now emulating the former colonials, toward the lingering control of international finance, the materialistic vision of a rising African elite, and the disappearance of moral standards and of a truly indigenous culture.

A Dream of Africa is indivisibly linked with *The Dark Child* not only because it is a chronological sequence to Camara Laye's first book but because it represents the hopes of a young man who left for France in order to acquire an education, returned to put this education to a useful task for his country's need and discovered then another side to the coin of independence. If *The Dark Child* evoked the memory of a maternal Africa, open to love and the sense of mystery, *A Dream of Africa* sketches the painful journey from ideal to reality, from the warm meaningful life of Kouroussa to the slum suburbs of Conakry where "poverty was common as dirt."

The action of the novel itself antedates independence by a few years. It comprises the intermediary period of the early 1950s when the former French African colonies were obtaining, through parliamentary pressure in Paris, some measure of autonomy, and when the control of certain internal affairs was gradually being passed into African hands. It should have been, for Fatoman the returning intellectual and his friend Konaté the young teacher, a period of hope, for "now it is we, and not the *colons*, who are directing the affairs of our land." Yet freedom was more nominal than virtual, for if the French granted some of the trappings of independence, they nonetheless retained actual control of the country so much so that "it *appears* to be our people directing affairs, but in actual fact it is still the *colons* in control." Considering the fact that this autobiographical novel was written *after* independence, one can see the boldness of Camara Laye's statement. For it is the present situation which he condemns through the oblique technique of time differential.

A Dream of Africa is frankly a political work. It dramatizes the emergence of a hedonistic African bougeoisie in the caricature of Bilali, the diamond trafficker, the *nouveau riche* whose measure of success and selfhood is the proud acquisition of a large American automobile, once custom-built for the President of Liberia. It demystifies the promises of education, still restrictive, still irrelevant to the deeper needs of a new nation. Konaté complains that no young promising African intellectual will, at the outset of his secondary school, be able to enter a university faculty. Fatoman at his return is everywhere confronted by the residuals of colonialism. The raw materials of the country— such as bauxite—are still being exploited by foreign companies. In contrast to the shabby dwellings of the Africans, there are the lovely villas inhabited by the administrative personnel of foreign companies. And with independence, many Africans have opted for this privileged style of living, undisturbed by the crying needs of the masses. Franz Fanon's analysis of this hard bourgeoisie, in *The Wretched of the Earth* is made alive in Camara Laye's novel.

If power had first meant a thrust for independence and the instrument to promote a socialist ideology, it has now become an end in itself. The doctrine is to be suavely injected into the veins of the masses through the rhetoric of party meetings, the opium of empty slogans and even more empty promises, the persuasion of the "Church, the Mosque and Fetishism." In the final analysis there remains, for Camara Laye, nothing but brute strength, violence to gag and destroy the opposition. Courageously Camara Laye identifies with his hero Fatoman, and takes upon himself the ungrateful task of unmasking the lies. There is no question who the "someone" is who must say, who must shout "that the violence you are now bringing into being in this land will be paid for by each of you, and especially by the innocent." It is the writer, the conscience of his society, who in Africa must take the first bold step.

The writer, the artist, what has become of him in this new society obsessed by material gain? Fatoman sees, with despair, that artisanship, local crafts, sculpture are dying out, being replaced by the cheap trinkets from India and the Middle East imported by the Lebanese merchants. Whoever has been confronted by the endless row of shops, whether in Dakar, Abidjan or Dar-es-Salaam, whether on an Avenue de l'Indépendence or Uhuru Street, confronted by these miniature bazaars stuffed with Indian ashtrays, plastic wallets and faked ebony statues, will understand the anger and sadness of Fatoman trying in vain to buy local handicraft. The African market now sells "nothing but junk."

There is much more than the artist's anger in Laye's outburst against the Lebanese merchants. Indirectly the writer raises the thorny question of minority groups living in Africa, within the core of African society, some remaining insular to the values and the needs of that society, while at the same time living by it, if not in some cases exploiting it. Similar attitudes have been expressed by East African writers vis-à-vis their own Asian community.

The disappearance of native crafts is but symptomatic of a spiritual atrophy. The cheap junk, the frippery and trash imported from Europe and the New World have replaced the once meaningful creations of the local African craftsmen and artists. Camara Laye returns to a privileged symbol of the past, that of his father, the smith, the sculptor, the representative of a humble yet magically empowered caste in Guinean society. In *The Dark Child* we recall the awe with which the young man watched his father work, and the creation which emerged from his hands was as much a product of artisan skill as of the spirits with whom his father's life was so intimately associated. In *A Dream of Africa* creation no longer arises from this harmony with the universe, for now man and the spirits of life are no longer in unison:

Though such powers have never entirely died out, my son, nevertheless I cannot conceal from you the sad fact that they have more or less lost their potency, and that it could hardly be otherwise considering the essential nature of our society which, although it did not break completely with its ancient beliefs, all the same allowed itself to be converted to Islam.

But the father does not confine himself to a theological argument, for he immediately adds:

And it is not so much that the ideas of power and mystery have died, have disappeared, as that the mystery and the power are no longer to be found where they used to be; for they are beginning to fade under the influence of modern ideas.

Camara Laye, deeply rooted, as most Africans are, in the traditional arts of Africa, bemoans the perversion of these in order to serve vague or greedy political needs. Surrounded as he was in his house in Conakry by his most cherished material possessions—if these could be called material!—masks, statues, recorded tapes of Sissoko playing the *cora*, Camara Laye came to feel that an essential part, perhaps the heart of African life, was being choked by the new utilitarian society.

And the image he gives us of that society, in the chapter called "Dramouss"—the title of the French edition of the book—is that of a nightmarish vision of cruel Kafkaesque dimension. Guinea, his beloved Guinea, is apprehended through a dream sequence as a penal colony where all the modern horrors of a concentration camp are being reenacted. Senseless cruelty is being perpetuated upon his compatriots by the brutish agents of a totalitarian state. It is only a dream. Yet, if Fatoman is finally rescued by the goddess Dramouss, we feel that it is a unique recuperation. There remains for his compatriots, as embodied in Camara Laye's didactic tableau, the task of promoting new ideals, new faith, supplemented by the honest working of a free people striving to achieve its full dignity and freedom:

I have also dreamed of a Lion, a great Black Lion, who saved us, who brought back prosperity to us, and who made all peoples his friends.

No amount of wishful thinking, abstract dreaming or the self-delusion of political rhetoric will satisfy both the material and spiritual needs of Camara Laye's people. The last image which Fatoman—and Camara Laye in his present exile in Senegal*—carries of Guinea is that of an aborted dream, the future compromised in his compatriots' hearts "because men had brought in doctrines which people were just swallowing wholesale like coconut milk."

A Dream of Africa is a bitter book. It is also a

*After years of governmental harassment Camara Laye was forced to exile himself from his homeland. He now lives in Dakar, Senegal. See Charles R. Larson, "Laye's Unfulfilled African Dream," in *Books Abroad*, XLIII (Spring, 1969), 209–211.

timely and courageous book, addressing itself no
longer to the idealization of a pre-colonial past nor to
the often repeated condemnation of colonialism, but to
the present political realities facing an independent
African state, indeed, if not facing any modern society.
It is above all the claims of a writer to investigate
freely his society and to become the witness of its
grandeur and limitations. At the center of Camara
Laye's harsh political assessment there is the need, the
obsession, to retain the privilege of lucidity.

Writing *A Dream of Africa* was a painful experience
for Camara Laye. It brought him no villa, no Mercedes-
Benz, no important title. It cost him his comfort, his
very security, his roots in the daily living of Guinea.
Yet it also insured that this novel will be read by those
among the younger generation of African intellectuals
who with Camara Laye share a love for the past, a
vision of a communal future and a sense of artistic
responsibility.

EMILE SNYDER

Conakry

I HAD LEFT Orly right in the middle of August, a month which, usually hot in Paris, was cool that year; not too sharp a coolness, but a coolness all the same (and I didn't care for it at all, I had never got completely used to it). And the plane, gaining altitude, had borne me up into a radiance in which I was already able to recognize the sky of my native land.

After six years, I was at last returning to my homeland; and ever since I had decided on this departure, my impatience had never ceased to grow; it was as if I were in the grip of a fever. For all those years which had kept me away were in fact years of exile; one's native land—whatever one does, and despite the generosity or the hospitality one finds in other countries— will always be something more than just a patch of earth: it is the Earth itself! It is one's family and one's friends, it is a familiar horizon and ways of life which the heart within one may well retain, but which it never willingly exposes to reality, never willingly surrenders over and over again to reality. At the end of this voyage, my great homeland was beckoning to me.

A brief stop at Dakar, and the plane was off again.

From then on, filled with an impatience I no longer tried to restrain, I began looking for the first sight of my native land. And soon after passing over the scattering of islands of so-called Portuguese Guinea, my native land appeared before me, low, very low, and not just because I was looking at it from the air, but because in that region it is land which has been virtually reclaimed from the sea: a land of lagoons, a red earth on which I could make out coconut palms, rice fields and the innumerable armies of mangrove trees that, at the edge of the continent, retain those acres of generous mud, a mud never weary of nourishing our harvests, a mud which itself is unceasingly nourished by the alluvia of countless rivers and streams.

To my left, the land gradually rose to become a country of lofty mountains; but I could do no more than imagine it: the eye would not carry so far, and even if my gaze had been able to reach the peaks of the range, it would have been lost in mists.

And then there took shape the island of green, the island of houses embowered in greenery, that is Conakry, at the extremity of the Kalum peninsula. Conakry! Conakry!

The plane was coming in to land. If I had been able to tear my eyes away from the town, perhaps I should have glimpsed in the distance the towering crest of Mount Kakulima, which stands at the neck of the peninsula; but I was unable to tear my eyes away; and when the town disappeared, the plane was already landing on the plain into which Kakulima's gentle foothills gradually subside.

I left the plane and gazed all about me, as if dumbfounded at having at last returned, after so many years. One landing strip is not much different from any other landing strip; it can never be anything more than a desolate expanse. But here there was that radiance, there was that brilliance of colors which belong only to that land, my native land, and which my eyes had grown unaccustomed to; a radiance more scintillating and more penetrative, a verdure more luxuriant and more fresh than anywhere else. My heart had not forgotten them, but my eyes . . . My eyes were dazzled! That freshness and that radiance belonged unmistakably to my Lower Guinea; as well as that humid warmth I was breathing in, and that sun flashing its spears of light!

I took the bus into town; it very soon reached the suburbs. There, poverty was common as dirt. At Madina and Dixinn in particular, dwellings were very rickety; they seemed to keep up by some sort of miracle; they displayed more of the art of the equilibrist than that of the architect.

'So these are the outskirts of Conakry!' my neighbor in the bus said in a low voice.

'Yes,' I replied in the same low voice. 'You don't seem too pleased about it.'

'No. There's nothing here. Absolutely not one single presentable dwelling or building! For that matter, the *colons* never wanted us to have anything presentable. They only think, and always did, of lining their wallets, in order to be able to spend delightful leaves in Europe. That's all the *colons* think of, not of the welfare of the African.'

'I don't agree with you,' I replied.

'What? You mean to say you're on the side of the *colons* now?'

'I'm not on anyone's side. I'm concerned with the truth. And besides I don't think the moment has yet come in which to condemn or blame the *colons*. That moment will come when we are able to prove, through our abnegation, through our work, through our concrete achievements, that we are superior to the *colons*.'

'No, no!' my fellow passenger repeated. 'Those people never did anything for us.'

'You must admit, all the same, my dear sir, that
colonization has given us a great deal.'

'No! It kept us back.'

'Kept us back! . . . Well, certainly, there were some
negative aspects, I admit, in colonialism. But when
everything's taken into consideration, the influence of
colonization on this country was beneficial.'

He fell silent, and from that moment never spoke to
me again. Meanwhile the old bus kept on rolling along,
and all the time there were places where the road
needed a bit of tar and gravel, where its innards were
laid bare—innards that were always rather rudimen-
tary. And almost everywhere, a drainage system that
relied a little too much on the pitch of the houses'
roofs; and too many unpaved roads, awash with mud
at that rainy season, but sheer dustbowls in the dry
season. The bus went rambling on; now it would turn
to the right, now to the left.

After half an hour I reached my relatives' house,
which is barely fifteen kilometers from the airport.
There I was re-united with my uncles and aunts. But
Marie? . . . Where was Marie? One of my aunts told
me that she was at a friend's house in the suburbs.
With wildly beating heart, I lay down on a bed.

What would I think of Marie now? Had she changed
at all with the years? I had left her in 1947. Was she
still, as formerly, calm and extraordinarily courageous?
Did she still have her feet on the ground? Was she still
just as much of a realist?

While these thoughts were flashing through my
mind, I heard a girl's voice. I got up at once and saw
standing on the threshold—Marie, even more beautiful, more bewitching, more disturbing than the picture
of her I had cherished in my memory.

For a few seconds we gazed at one another without

a word, as if we were indifferent to one another, or as if, through timidity, we were fearful of displaying our feelings in the presence of my aunts, who were always looking for a chance to tease us. But then, forgetting those importunate intruders, and obeying an identical impulse, the impulse of our souls and hearts suddenly aflame, we suddenly found ourselves in one another's arms.

Marie and I hardly said a word for hours; it was because our joy at being re-united after so many years was beyond speech and understanding. At the rare moments when my aunts left us alone, we contented ourselves with exchanging smiles or even holding hands . . .

Even after that, at the midday meal, our conversation was superficial: it was restricted to harmless subjects. But soon, when I started talking about my experiences in Europe, I sensed that Marie was mischievously avoiding all reference to her own life. After she had left the table, I followed her to her room and gave her a questioning glance. I wanted to know everything, without delay: what her life had been like in Dakar, how the people there had treated her, and above all, whether she had remained faithful to me . . . When she saw me enter, she lowered her head, and for a while a heavy silence hung over us. I pulled her by the arm.

'Come on, let's go for a walk.'

'I'll get my scarf.'

Still keeping silence, we set off in the direction of the town, intending to visit various districts, but going by way of the corniche. The breeze played with Marie's scarf. I lit a cigarette, and, afraid of offending her, I refrained from asking her questions about ourselves, about our friendship, about our promises to one another. 'I'll wait for the psychological moment.' I thought to myself. 'I mean, the moment when our timidity has been completely banished, and then slip into the conversation a few words concerning our personal problems.'

'Everything's changed so much,' I said tentatively.

'Everything's changed,' she agreed. 'Over there, on the islands, there are big warehouses now, for the bauxite ore . . . And villas, too. Splendid ones. But they are not for people like you and me . . . They belong to the foreign companies,' she ended, with a burst of laughter.

'Yes,' I agreed, 'that's true. Is this the road to Donka? When we were little, the town was a long, long way from Dixinn.'

'It's getting quite an important place now!'

At Tumbo Bridge, on the road out of town, I saw before me the Conakry-Niger railway. But a little further on there appeared to be another line.

'Are there two lines?' I asked.

'It's the same old story,' she said. 'The story of the foreign companies. The second line belongs to the Mining Company.'

At present we were walking along the Niger road, turning our backs on the Tumbo Bridge. We were entering the town from the sea; but at first I could hardly recognize the place. Certainly these were the avenues and the boulevards I had left behind, and the same trees; but at almost every point there were no longer the same buildings. I may have remembered a few of them. But I was seeing others, many others, for the first time. When we arrived in the center of the town we were tired of walking. Worn out, I hailed a taxi. But it was already too far away and the driver did not hear my call.

I had hailed him automatically, as I would have done in Paris. But suddenly I realized that calling a taxi, at that place in Conakry, was something quite new.

'Are you surprised to see taxis in Conakry? We too are quite up-to-date,' said Marie.

'Yes, progress comes slowly but surely . . . But the town is small.'

'It certainly is small, and cramped. We have just walked all round it in less than two hours. To make up for the lack of modern houses, Providence has luckily provided us with greenery. Just think how peaceful the view was from the corniche!'

'It's a magnificent view!' I replied.

'I hear that over there, in Paris, it's very beautiful. But that it's very cold!'

'It's very cold over there. So cold that, living here, you can't possibly imagine what it's like.'

'Here it will soon begin to rain tremendously hard. There's a rainfull of at least four meters. Believe me, nothing has really changed since your departure; this season still well deserves the name of rainy season. We are now in August, but the season begins in June and finishes in October or November,' she added. 'I'm warning you, because you never spent your summer holidays in Conakry, I'm warning you that you'd better pack your suits in your case, because just now the rain comes down in cataracts. A real deluge, which leaves the sky, if not absolutely pure, at least fairly clear.'

'Thank you, teacher,' I said smiling. 'You're telling me a lot of things I knew nothing about.'

She burst out laughing, satisfied, it appeared, by the compliments I had just made her.

By now she was completely relaxed; I seized this opportunity to lead our conversation toward our personal concerns; toward those problems which we both had very much at heart.

'Well, now,' I ventured, 'perhaps we can speak about us, now.'

But scarcely had I uttered this phrase than she lowered her head, as if embarrassed by the thought of soon seeing the veil lifted on her past; that past to which, just recently, she had refused to make any allusion at all; suddenly she became again the timid young girl, the secretive young girl, whom once I knew. Nevertheless, she replied coldly:

'Perhaps.'

Had the love she had once felt for me vanished? The impulse we had experienced a little while ago, that common impulse of our souls and our hearts—had it been a sincere impulse, or just a pretended one? I reminded myself that when we had been parted, she going to Dakar and I to Paris, the intervals between our letters had often been lengthy, and that (I went on musing) had probably happened in direct proportion to the increasing frequency of Marie's dates with other boys; or else that, her love for them becoming steadily deeper, and her heart dedicated, completely dedicated, to other boys, she no longer had any feeling for me: she no longer loved me!

All kinds of gloomy thoughts shadowed my spirits, even though I had no real reason to feel sad.

'I should not have come back. My presence in Conakry makes you unhappy! . . . I had expected it. So, before coming, I took the precaution of buying a return ticket. I shall go back tomorrow,' I said.

Then, suddenly, examining her face, I sensed that my doubts had no foundation, that my arguments were false; but however absurd and mistaken they were, they seemed to me to be the only ones capable of forcing Marie to lift the veil on her life, or more exactly on that portion of her life of which I knew nothing. As if to convince me of her sincerity, she raised her head and looked at the sky, then fixed her eyes on a point just above my head, as if she had discovered something up there, as if she had found there the answer she had to give me. And she protested, vigorously:

'I do not want you to go back!'

If she's against my departure, it's because she still loves me, I said to myself.

'Oh, really?' I said, feigning surprise.

'Yes!'

And she went on softly:

'It was a shock when I received your letter. I knew all the time that you would finally come back. You and I are both now passing through the moment I was so afraid of. But I'm glad that the moment has come.'

In my inmost heart, I thought to myself: 'She has not forgotten my relations with Françoise.'—That girl, that slip of a girl who, from France, had sent letters harassing my parents, pressing them to give their consent to our marriage.

'If it's Françoise you're talking about, I must tell you that I finished with her long ago. Anyhow, to me she was nothing more than someone to talk to; I mean, someone I quite liked, and with whom I exchanged ideas, with the sole aim of giving each other information about ways of life in our respective countries. When are you going to forget all that? When are you going to put the past behind you, and fix your eyes on the future?'

'Forget!' she said softly, stressing each syllable separately. 'Naturally, thousands of boys deceive their fiancée!'

'But what other answer could I possibly have given you?' I murmured. 'I'm telling you that all that is over and done with now. And what would you say if I were to marry two, three or even four wives, the number permitted by our sacred book, the Koran?'

I said that to tease her. But the phrase irritated her and she flew off the handle.* She began to shout.

'If that's what you've got in mind, let me tell you right away that my answer is no! No, no! *That* you'll never do! D'you hear me? . . . Never! . . . Either I'm the one woman under your roof, or not at all. Let that be thoroughly understood and digested, once and for all!'

'Don't get worked up, Marie. You shall be the one

---

*In the original, translated from a Malinké idiom meaning literally 'to fly out of its sheath' (presumably of a sword). (*Translator's note*)

and only woman under my roof . . . Didn't you understand I was joking?'

'All right! . . . That's settled! . . . If it's a joke, then
that's all right. But one never knows with you men.
You say many a true word in jest! . . . Then you
understand?' she said, returning to the theme closest to
her heart. 'I was beginning to think there was no longer
any place for me.'

'I'm listening, Marie.'

She looked at me. Perhaps she wanted to observe the
effect that these words produced on me. It was probably not the effect she expected. She steadied her voice
and continued:

'It's difficult for you men to understand us women.'

'All the same, you ought to try to make me understand.'

We had gone out at two o'clock, and now six o'clock
had just struck from the Cathedral tower. We were
strolling back to the corniche. I lit another cigarette
and suggested to Marie that we should sit down on a
bench.

She sat down beside me, very close beside me; our
hips were touching. My heart was beating wildly, very
wildly. All my heart and all my soul were yearning
toward her, as if magnetized by a sublime and indefin-
able passion. I looked at her: she was more serene and
beautiful than ever. The gently blowing breeze, inten-
sifying my happiness, played with her scarf, whose
ends waved on her shoulders. She wanted to talk, but I
should have liked her to keep quiet. My thoughts suddenly took wings. Now they would alight upon the
future I was imagining, a future full of joy, now upon
the past, then on the present . . . And soon they were
mingled with the infinite; they soared very high, infinitely high. I wanted to tell Marie: 'You're lovely,' but
I restrained myself. A force more powerful than my
own will, and the sudden thought that life does not

always fit in with the plans we have made for it, snatched me from my reveries and obliged me to listen to her.

'It was a nightmare,' she was saying. 'At first, I heard that you had married. And then that your wife was writing regularly to your family. And so on and so on! . . . One day, I felt so much pain that they made me enter Ballay Hospital, where I stayed I don't know how long. The poor doctors kept taking my temperature and looking after me. But my sickness was mental rather than physical. Only psychiatrists could have cured me.'

She was silent for a while, then went on:

'But one day, the veil half-lifted; I told myself: "What's the use? He's married!" As if giving me a chance to revenge myself (it was not, nor could it be, anything but a pretense of vengeance), Hady came to the house, and I let him keep coming . . . If the truth be known, every time I saw him I wanted to scream. It's funny, when a girl doesn't love a boy! . . . So then I asked the good Lord to let the veil fall over my mind again, I implored him to make me a child again, to give back to me the carefree heart of a child, so that I might be incapable of remembering the past.'

'Calm down, now,' I said with a guilty air. 'Calm down, I beg of you! All that is finished. Yes, over and done with.'

She released my hand, stood up, then dried with the end of her scarf eyes that had suddenly filled with tears. All at once I felt a lump in my throat, but I did not weep. Can a man weep in front of a young girl? . . . The tears of men are horrible; unlike the tears of women, most often they never flow; my tears, instead of flooding my eyes, had flooded the innermost recesses of my being, my conscience itself.

She moved away from me, and, leaning on one of the low walls of the corniche, gazed, as did many visi-

tors to the place, out in the direction of the Islands of
Loos. The setting sun, turning deep red, suspended still
by invisible threads above those islands, was now sending out rays less powerful than those which had greeted
our arrival. Silently I moved across to the wall of the
corniche. Each man and each woman leaning there
was silent too. Each and every one seemed animated by
an intense inner life, and this intensity was such that
no one spoke a word, for each and every one was
giving free rein to reverie . . .

But what could they be thinking of, all those men
and all those women?

Were they thinking of the islands that barred the
horizon before us?

And those men of Europe, those Europeans, surrounded by their women and their children, leaning
just like the Africans on the wall of the corniche, and
even more silent than the Africans—what were they
dreaming of?

Were they thinking of their native land, of the leave
they would spend in their native land, after a tour of
two years? I expect so.

I went up to Marie, I softly uttered her name. As she
did not reply, I took hold of her blouse and shook her;
but her eyes remained fixed upon the immensity of the
ocean, and so she appeared to be very far away.

What could she be thinking of? Probably of the
many years she had spent in Senegal, staying with her
guardians, who had made much of her in such a kind
and pleasant way. And perhaps she was also thinking
of what my life in Paris had been like? Both things
were in her mind, certainly; that could be guessed from
the tense look on her face. As she was no longer aware
of my presence, I withdrew from her a little, from her
countenance that was now radiant, now sad. That sadness betrayed the condition of a soul poisoned by jealousy; a jealousy that could not be admitted, against my
former life, and more precisely against a girl who, nev-

ertheless, had never been anything more to me than a
'guardian.'

I was now, as she was, standing in an angle of the
wall. The sea seemed tempestuous; the tide was coming
in and the waves, like white battering-rams, came
galloping toward us and crashing against the shore
with the sound of a storm in the forest. After having
smashed itself against the rocks, this roaring would be
transformed into thousands of little noises which, as
the waves drew them further and further back from the
shore, would dissolve and melt into a pastoral sym-
phony, with its balaphons and coras, its flutes and its
tom-toms. And it was a perpetual movement. The
white horses would now dash themselves upon the
rocks, now gallop far away from the shore. And when,
suddenly, emerging from my reverie, I turned round, I
saw Marie standing close beside me. Had she, too,
finally emerged from her darkling dreams? Had she
come back from Paris and Senegal?

'Forget the past!' I said, taking her arm. 'That's the
greatest favor you could do me.'

'I must tell you. You are forgiven, but, don't you
see, I simply must talk to you about it. I suffered
terribly at the time, you know! I was with my relations,
thinking that the family atmosphere might dull my
thoughts. I spent hours going round with my friends.
But often I stayed at home, languishing away . . .
There was nothing to be done: "Fatoman . . . Married!
. . . Paris." It was as if those three words were the only
ones remaining in my brain.'

Standing behind her, I drew her close to me with a
sudden access of tenderness. As if unable to hold out
any longer, she returned my embrace and laid her head
back on my shoulder. She was silent for a moment. I
realized that she had finally shaken off all those things
that had so painfully tormented her during the past
years. We were both moved . . .

'Let's go back now, Marie,' I whispered. 'It's getting

late. How I wish I could have been beside you at that
moment when they made you believe that I'd got married!'

Hand in hand, we walked slowly back to our dwelling place, continuing our conversation all the time. In
more tranquil tones, for her agony was now almost
over, she went on with her story.

'I know *you'd* have done anything,' she said. 'But at
the time, no one—do you realize?—no one could help
me! There are certain struggles which one can only
deal with alone. Finally I took a job as mistress at a
boarding school. From the time I finished my studies, I
became absorbed in that work body and soul. And it
was just what I needed: a position in which I was
constantly on the go, day and night almost, supervising
those girls, the majority of whom were already awakened, or beginning to be awakened to life. I would give
some of them advice, and punish others who over-
stepped the mark. In fact, I had such responsibilities
that I was left no time to think of my own troubles. I
was always intending to write to you, and indeed I
began to write perhaps as many as two hundred letters;
but the thought that you had been unfaithful to me
exasperated me and I always gave up. You did well to
return, Fatoman.'

'I am very happy to be with you again, and to know
that it is all over now, that all your anxieties are al-
layed.'

We were approaching the house. It was dark already. At the sight of us, my aunts burst out laughing.
I went to take refuge in my room. Marie certainly did
the same, for I could no longer see her in the concession.

'Marie, Fatoman, come and eat!' my Aunt Awa
shouted.

'Always the same!' I thought. 'She cannot leave us
alone! Every time she has to shout our names, the
whole family has to hear those two names at the same

time, when all we two want is to live quietly and discreetly.' As neither of us answered, her voice rang out again.

'Whether you answer me or no, you'll both eat together from tonight on. We've had quite enough of this intolerable bashfulness!'

Then, addressing the children:

'Go on! Go and play outside, or take yourselves off for a walk. Your cousin and his girl are going to dine in this room.'

'Let them stay, aunt,' I said. 'I like having them around.'

'I know you like having them around. But I also know that you will raise no bite of food to your lips as long as there are people around you. The same with your girl. Oh! Talk about bashful!'

Finally we got through the meal.

'You know,' I began, 'life over there isn't easy.'

'In Paris?'

'Yes. When one has no allowance from the State or from one's parents, life is difficult. I'm just wondering if it wouldn't be wiser for you to wait for me here in Guinea. In two or three years' time we could meet again and get married.'

'In two or three years!' she echoed.

Just at that moment, my Uncle Mamadou entered our room and Marie told him of my fears.

'Fatoman,' he addressed me. 'Why have we consented to your union? Why have I given my personal approval to it? Because I know that Marie is a simple-hearted girl, born of a simple-hearted family. And from my own personal experience, from having lodged and fed her in my house for many years I know that she has always been satisfied to accept, with good grace, whatever your "little mothers"* offered her. During all this time, she has led a modest existence,

*'Little mothers' is a Malinké expression meaning aunts. (*Translator's note*)

without envying her more fortunate associates . . . I would advise you, and advise you again and again, to be quite sure you realize all this.'

'Very well, uncle. But over there, it's cold. Clothes will have to be paid for, the room, my college fees, so much has to be paid for, and with what? I don't expect to receive a study scholarship from the State. All my efforts to obtain one have been in vain. Life is hard over there, uncle.'

'Well, that's too bad! You're trying to tell me that Marie will die of hunger over there,' he said, laughing. 'But she'll go everywhere with you. She will appreciate all the more the future happiness of you both from having largely contributed to it herself. And then it is perhaps the best way, I might even venture to say the only way, for her to prove to herself that she is marrying you neither for position nor money. Finally, you must get it into your head that you are not dealing with some middle-class woman, but with a girl who, like yourself, is a daughter of the common people.'

In my uncle's way of thinking (for he was a very religious person), a man's success in life could not be assured simply by his own unaided efforts; those efforts had to be supported by God himself. According to Uncle Mamadou, God always provides sustenance for all the mouths he has created. So that, in his view, looking after Marie's needs was more God's affair than mine.

Such faith in God and in the principles of the Koran being unshakable, no argument, however brilliant, could make my Uncle Mamadou retract a statement he had pondered so long.

'Very well, uncle,' I said.

'That's the way,' Marie replied, highly satisfied. '*Tonton* Mamadou knew what was in my heart, what I wanted to express.'

'Actually, my boy,' my uncle said, 'your father-in-law, before leaving us to take up his new post, insisted that the religious ceremonies for your marriage should take place. We have already been through these formalities at the Mosque. As for the civil marriage, you can do it whenever you like. It's not difficult; all you have to do is to present yourselves at some town hall before the mayor or some other official.'

He was silent a moment. He became grave. After having put a piece of kola in his mouth, he went on, slowly chewing the nut (his jaws moving like those of a ruminating goat):

'I am therefore happy to inform you that from this night on, from this very moment in which I am speaking to you, on the orders of your father-in-law and with the approval of all of us, Marie will become your wife. From now on you are united in the eyes of God and in the eyes of men. And may I add that you must come to an understanding now, in order that you may be able to spend your time here in the pleasantest way possible. I hereby command you to live, from this night on, as man and wife. You may occupy the room belonging to my young brother Sékou until such time as you are ready to take your departure for fresh adventures, for life after all is nothing but a series of adventures. This, Fatoman, is the pleasant surprise which I have felt it my right and my duty to reveal unto you.'

That moment of the announcement of my marriage was a moving one. So now I was provided with a better half! . . . After his oration, my Uncle Mamadou withdrew and left us alone with our thoughts.

'Are you satisfied, Fatoman?' Marie asked.

'Yes, very satisfied. Are you?'

'I am the happiest woman in the world. Will you give me permission, my beloved husband,' she went on, her face radiant, 'to go and acquaint a girl friend of mine with the news?'

'What? You're going out so late?'

'Ah, you're jealous, is that it?' she said.

'No. What's that got to do with it?'

'I have been told that a husband who is not jealous does not love his wife.'

'Who told you such a thing?'

'A girl friend,' she replied, laughing.

'One can love and still not show jealousy. It's all a question of temperament.'

'Then will you kindly tell me why *you* are not jealous?' she insisted.

'I am one of those who readily trust in others. As I am a fairly serious person myself, I trust you, whereas an old petticoat-chaser could never trust his wife. He believes that she, once she is out of his sight, will inevitably behave in the same way as himself. And then . . . Oh, no, it would take too long to explain it all to you!'

'No! Go on and explain what you mean! I'm interested to hear,' she cried, very excited.

'No, Marie, it would take too long. But if such be your desire, on our arrival in Kouroussa I shall ask our witch doctor Kessery to describe to you the adventures of a jealous man, and you'll see they're not at all pleasant.'

'I'm dying to hear all about them,' she said. 'I'm longing to go there and find good "cowrie-shell players." '*

She stood up suddenly, shoving back her chair; I could see that she was restless and anxious to go out.

'Let's go for a walk. We'll go and visit my friend Aminata, whose husband is a trade unionist. It'll be a chance to get to know them better.'

'Wherever you like, Madame!'

I was weary and I would dearly have liked to lie down and sleep, but I did not dare say so to her; until

*Malinké phrase meaning fortunetellers. (*Translator's note*)

that moment, my temperament had been that of a confirmed bachelor, and I used to get up and go to bed whenever the fancy took me; I had led a somewhat topsy-turvy existence. All the same, I was now giving up my independence with surprising facility and rapidity, and becoming the most exemplary of husbands.

'Well, my girl, are you ready?'

And I followed her out. I would have followed her anywhere. I did not want to provoke her. If one has any dignity at all, one should not provoke a girl who marries you without bothering to find out whether you are rich or poor, and who moreover declares herself ready to follow you even into the jaws of hell.

'Yes, I'm ready. Hurry up,' she cried.

We went to the house of Aminata, whose husband, voluble and intelligent, sketched for me, hour after hour, a picture of the political situation. The demands of certain *colons*, the quarrels between the parties, the lot . . .

Finally, at midnight, when our eyelids were weighed down with slumber, Aminata and her husband brought us back to our house in their car.

'Do not forget that from now on we are authorized to live together in connubial felicity,' I reminded Marie, as we entered the gate of Uncle Mamadou's concession.

My Aunt Khadi, who was in bed, but who always goes to sleep very late, overheard my words and called out in support of what I had said:

'Marie! Marie! Don't you go making any difficulties!' she shouted, teasingly. 'I've no room for you here in my bedchamber,' she added. 'And besides, my couch is too narrow for the two of us. You'd be far better off staying in there beside your husband.'

Marie came in and sat down bashfully on the foot of the bed. I pretended not to have noticed her entry.

'Let us pray,' I said.

'Pray?'

'Yes. Did not our Creator fashion us in order to pray?'

'Only to pray?'

'Yes, my dear. All the other creatures are fashioned by him for our pleasure, but we, we are fashioned by him in order to pray and to render thanks unto him for all his mercies.'

'But who, *him*?'

'The good Lord.'

'You're right, Fatoman. I too like to have a quiet think now and then.'

And in the dead of night, now kneeling, now bowing my forehead to the ground, I prayed, with her at my side.

After the traditional Salam Alaikum, she ventured to say:

'I prefer to lie on the outside of the bed, so you will take the side next to the wall.'

'As you wish.'

'Don't put out the light.'

'Just as you like,' I said, to quiet her.

With the bedclothes tucked in round me, I was now in bed, with her beside me, very close beside me. I don't think we talked very long. I soon dropped off and slept like a log. . . .

'Take a good rest, my children. Enjoy yourselves,' Uncle Mamadou told us when we awoke, before leaving for his office.

I took the opportunity to make several excursions in the neighborhood of Conakry; accompanied by Marie, naturally. We went to the Islands of Loos, which I had seen the night before from the corniche. These islands are situated about two nautical miles from Conakry, slightly to the south. From the corniche, one looks straight down on the island of Kassa. It is a long narrow island, a simple strip of earth, slightly undulating, whose luminous green stands out sharply against the nacreous deep. And it is really this island which sets off the sea, shows it to its best advantage, in a way that cannot be appreciated when its uniform billows stretch away uninterrupted to the horizon. Behind this strip of earth there is another, Tamara, whose northern point one can just see. Each island forms an arc of a circle. At the center there is an islet, the island of Roume. These islands, according to the experts, are of the same volcanic nature as the Island of Tumbo, on which Conakry is built.

That first morning, we went to Kassa, the nearest island. We took our seats on the *pétrolette*.* As we drew nearer, we made out the warehouses on the shore.

'Look, dear. Is that where the foreign companies have their installations?'

'Yes, that's what I was telling you about, don't you remember, the day you arrived?'

'Just look behind you. How beautiful our capital is!'

She did as I asked and Conakry was revealed to her, with its tall houses rising out of the tropical greenery, with its coconut palms and mangrove trees.

'Oh, yes, it's beautiful!' she cried. 'It's magnificent! It's like one of those places in Florida you see at the pictures!'

'Yes, it's an African Florida. Closer than the one in America, for film directors in search of location shots. Perhaps one day there will be more houses, for the country's riches will be fully exploited.

'It will take us some time,' I went on, 'to turn our country into an ultra-modern land. But it will come, one day! . . .'

'*Aminâl Aminâl Aminâl*'*

The *pétrolette* finally tied up at the quayside, and we

*Longboat with outboard motor. (*Translator's note*)
*Malinké for 'So be it!' (*Translator's note*)

disembarked. On that island, inhabited by our compatriots, Canadians and Frenchmen had built their own city next to the native village. The whole place had a very fine appearance, the appearance of a garden city. There was lots of space. An excellent road ran the whole length of the island. A bus service linked the various centers of population.

Marie and I met the engineer in charge, who explained things to us:

'Bauxite comes to the surface at numerous points on the Islands of Loos. Here it does not appear on the surface, but is covered by only a layer of earth, generally very thin, mostly vegetable mold. It is cleared away by bullodzers.'

'Is this a profitable concern?'

'Yes. Bauxite can be exploited commercially everywhere on the islands. It's practically open-cast production. The ore is dynamited and loaded by mechanical shovels.'

And indeed, as we proceeded with the engineer to visit every corner of the island, we saw for ourselves that the exploitation of bauxite here could be carried out with ease once the deposits had been located by meticulous and repeated borings and careful analysis of fragments brought to the surface. This task has to be carried out with great precision; and it is indispensable if errors are to be avoided.

'What is bauxite, sir?' Marie asked.

'It is a weathering of surface rocks,' he explained. 'And Guinea possesses an inexhaustible stock of it. But in order to reduce transport costs the ore is washed, to rid it of its impurities, chiefly silicon, at the refining plant here in Kassa.'

'May we see how this plant operates?' inquired Marie, who was curious by nature.

A short distance away and close to the embarkation quay we entered the plant which crushed, washed and dried the ore. The most impressive item here was the cylindrical rotary drying oven. When the bauxite came out it was carried on moving belts to the stockage silos, in the same way that it would finally be carried aboard the cargo boats.

'Thank you very much,' I said to the engineer, 'for having shown us all this, and for having taught us so many things we did not know about the islands.'

So we said good-bye to him and to the island of Kassa, and we took our seats again on board the *pétrolette,* which once more began to glide over the sea; it was calm that day, and the little waves hardly touched the sides of the boat with their weak caresses.

'Are you satisfied with your day?' Uncle Mamadou asked on our return.

'Oh, yes, uncle, very satisfied. We visited Kassa. It's magnificent out there.'

I was interrupted by Aunt Awa, who said: 'I should like to see how Marie has arranged her husband's bed-chamber.'

At these words, the whole family broke out laughing. Marie ran away; my aunt went to fetch her back and made her sit in an armchair. Marie lowered her head.

'Raise your head,' sighed Aunt Awa, 'and look me straight in the eyes.'

Everyone in the room again began to roar with laughter. Aunt Awa went on, in an ironic tone of voice:

'Tell me, Fatoman, does she give your back a good massage at night, before going to sleep?'

'No, she doesn't,' I said, laughing.

'Well, then,' she went on vehemently, 'what do the pair of you do with yourselves when you're alone?'

'Oh,' I said, 'I read newspapers and novels. While I'm doing that, she turns her back on me and curls up like a cat.'

The laughter broke out again, even louder.

'That is not the way to go about things,' Aunt Awa informed me. 'You should talk and amuse yourselves, and not turn your backs on one another. Do you understand what I mean?'

'Yes,' I answered eagerly. 'That's what I've always wanted. But she remains indifferent . . .'

'Well, now, Marie!' Aunt Awa cried, bursting out laughing, 'what's this about you being indifferent to Fatoman?'

After a short silence, Marie, her head lowered, replied bashfully:

'I'm ashamed in front of him.'

'Oh!' my aunt replied. 'You'll soon get over that. One month from now at the very latest, we shall see whether you're still as bashful. And please tell me, Marie, how many children do you count on having? . . . Nine, I suppose, like your mother?'

When she heard this last remark, Marie tried to escape once more, but Aunt Awa caught her just before she reached the door, and went on teasing her:

'Don't run away. Tell me how many children you're going to have.'

'I don't know,' she replied.

'Well, then,' retorted my aunt, 'we don't want all that many. We want very few children, d'you understand?'

'Yes,' whispered Marie. 'But what have you in mind when you say very few children? Could you give me a figure?'

'We want no more than seven!'

'Oh, no! Seven children! It's far too many!'

By this time they were all splitting their sides with laughter.

'Well, anyhow,' put in my Uncle Sékou. 'Tell us at least how many girls and how many boys?'

'But I never said anything about that!' she cried.

'Silence means consent,' my Uncle Sékou retorted.

At that moment my Uncle Mamadou entered the room.

'It's getting late,' he said, in a commanding voice. 'Let the young couple alone. Don't bother them too much. Let each one go to his or her own room.'

'Wouldn't it be wise, uncle, isn't it time for me to pay a visit to your brother? I expect he has heard of my return. And perhaps he is anxious to see me.'

As if speaking approvingly of such a brusque departure, he replied:

'Good. Very well, my boy. To save time, you could take the *Heron** tomorrow morning. From Kankan, a taxi will soon take you to Kouroussa. You'll be there before noon. And you, my dear,' he said, turning toward Marie, 'you shall go with you husband. It will be the very best opportunity for you to become acquainted with your father-in-law's family. Go quickly, my children, but come back soon. We haven't yet had enough of you. And also, I should like to personally keep an eye on the early stages of your marriage, to observe how you both conduct yourselves. Go quickly! If you delay, I shall send Aunt Awa after you,' he ended, with a burst of laughter.

'I know, uncle, that you would like to keep an eye on us,' I said. 'But my time is limited. I was only able to get two weeks' leave. I should like to return to Dakar by way of Bamako. So tomorrow, instead of taking the *Heron*, we shall take the train.'

'As you wish, my boy. Do not forget to greet my brother and his family for me in Kouroussa. And when you have returned to Paris, write to me often. But this evening, I should like you to go and say your farewells to your mother-in-law.'

So that evening I went to the district called Almamya, where my mother-in-law lived.

*Small eight-seater airplane used for transportation to the interior of the Colony.

'Leaving already?' she cried when she saw me.

'Yes. It is the time for your daughter to leave you, with your gracious permission. I have come to take her,' I replied, using courteous forms of speech.

'Do you hear that, Marie?' she said, turning to her daughter. 'You are going on a magnificent journey with Fatoman. You are going to leave us now, and follow your husband whithersoever he goes! This journey will be even more wonderful than the one you made to Senegal some years ago.'

The smell of onion and fried chicken, which I like very much, scented the courtyard; the smell followed us right into the parlor where we had sat down . . .

'I don't want to go, mama,' Marie protested. 'I want to stay here with you.'

'Come, come, my daughter! Be reasonable. The days are over when you could stay with your mother all the time. At your age, your place is no longer here. It is at your husband's side. At first, you were glad to be leaving with him. What's happened? Don't you love him any more?'

'Oh, yes, mama,' she answered. 'But I want to stay here with you.'

'You must go. Now, now, my daughter, take courage.'

Marie began to weep . . . And she was still in tears the next day, when we went to take the train. Her mother was with us, as well as my aunts and my uncles. The train whistle blew, and perhaps it might even have set off with my mother-in-law in the compartment if the guard, a young man in khaki uniform and wearing a peaked cap, had not come to give her a tap on the shoulder, warning her that it was time to leave the train.

After she had kissed us on both cheeks, swallowing back her sobs, she got down on the platform, and, not wishing to be lost among the crowd, with her short stature, she kept her place well in front of everyone in that crowd, a good part of whom were weeping. She stood motionless, her head always lifted, never for one single moment taking her eyes from the compartment in which we had taken our seats.

For a brief instant we lost sight of her. The passengers had all boarded the train, now packed to bursting point. Finally, just as the train was beginning to draw out, my eyes encountered those of my mother-in-law. She was running along the railway track, endeavoring to retain the image of our smiling faces as long as possible. I was laughing. But Marie could only give her mother a strained, anguished smile. Standing beside her, I held my wife tenderly round the shoulders, so that she might feel some comfort in her distress, and through the window, we waved our last adieus. The motley, shifting crowd remained visible until the first bend in the track. The train, insensible to our grief, continued its inexorable course across the plains of Lower Guinea.

We were already approaching Kindia.

'Do you know this town, Marie?'

'Not properly . . . I just passed through it in a car on the way to Télimélé, my native village.'

'I know this town well, and personally I like it very much. It's not far from Conakry, you see. Three hours, and one is there.'

'Three hours,' she added, 'because there are mountains to be skirted, hills to ascend. And also, there are long halts at various stations. Otherwise, one could go much more quickly. Kindia is a magnificent spot.'

'Didn't you feel the change in climate? It's less oppressively hot up here.'

'I noticed,' she replied, 'that as we approached Kouria, the difference could be distinctly felt. One feels one is in a more temperate climate than at Conakry.'

'You'll see, when we reach Kindia station, it's a real

crossroads at which we shall find all the ethnic types in our country. And did you know that we can buy bananas there almost for nothing?'

'Do they come from Kindia, the bananas we get in Conakry?'

'Not all,' I replied, 'but most of them.'

'Kindia appeals to me already, because of what you've been telling me.'

'One day, Marie, I promise you we'll go to Pastoria, where the monkeys will amuse you. The snakes too.'

'Oh, snakes! . . . I shall never go to Pastoria. I have a horror of snakes,' she declared, with a disgusted look.

'There's nothing to be afraid of, Marie. The snake pit is surrounded by a deep ditch, so that the reptiles cannot reach anyone outside.'

'I don't like snakes,' she insisted. 'It makes me sick when I see a snake.'

'Very well, then, I shall take you way up there, right up that mountain you can see in front of us,' I offered. 'It's the highest in the range surrounding Kindia.'

'Oh, yes, I like mountains. I like being high up and having a bird's-eye view, an immense and magnificent panorama.'

'From the summit, when there are no clouds, one can see Conakry and a good stretch of coastline. You can even feel the earth actually turning. You have the physical sensation of that rotatory effect. You feel you are turning, that we are all turning, turning with the globe.'

'Yes!' she cried. 'Our land is magnificent!'

I was still seated next to her on the seat in our first-class compartment. The breeze swept the interior, blowing in through the wide-open windows; it caressed and refreshed our countenances.

'Will we soon be arriving at Kindia?' she inquired.

'Yes, soon.'

One hour later, indeed, our train stopped in the station of Kindia, but the halt was a short one and once again we began to roll on and on and on. Gradually Marie fell asleep. The line was approaching the Futa Jalon mountains with their bare summits and their flanks covered with a dense jungle growth. The train moved down a wooded valley, traversed the laterite spurs, went puffing across savannahs, plains, the vast plains of the Niger. Night had already fallen when we stopped at Kouroussa Station.

I roused Marie.

'It's a long journey, isn't it?' I said, trying to dissipate her lassitude with conversation.

We were now walking along the street, our luggage being carried on the heads of porters.

'It's long, but it's not unpleasant to make such a journey by train. I slept all day. Didn't you?' she said, yawning.

'No, I didn't sleep a wink.'

'Didn't you even have a short nap?'

'No.'

'Insomnia?' she asked, anxiously.

'I don't know. Perhaps.'

Staring me in the face, she was endeavoring to find out . . .

'I believe you are one of those men who are afraid of heights,' she declared.

'No, I'm not afraid, although I am not a mountain dweller like you. Why should I be afraid?' I added, with a guilty look.

We had been walking, walking quite a long way, preceded by our two bearers, before I finally glimpsed the straw roofs of our native huts.

'Fatoman, you're not telling me the truth!' she cried.

And as I lowered my head, she realized that she had guessed correctly. She burst out laughing.

'At every precipice we came to, Marie,' I finally avowed, 'it seemed to me that my last moment had come, that the train was going to topple into the ravine and that death was about to swoop down upon me.'

'But death is everywhere!' she replied, with another burst of laughter. 'It strikes you down wherever it likes, even in your own bedchamber. One cannot escape from it.'

'I'm sure of that, but in the train, every time I cross the Futa, every time I gaze down into the ravines from the mountain heights, it is impossible for me not to be afraid . . . Oh, you would have split your sides laughing, if you'd seen me as we were rounding the precipices.'

'What happened?' she asked, highly amused.

'Every time we traveled round a precipice, I kept trying desperately, by pulling on the seat, to keep our carriage on the tracks.'

'Stop romancing!'

We were still walking, but we were already inside the village, making our way down the silent lanes.

'So Kouroussa men can't be very spunky!' she went on in a mocking voice. 'It's out in the bush, Kouroussa!'

'If Kouroussa is in the bush,' I countered, 'what about your own village, Télimélé? . . . That's virgin forest!'

'No, that's not true, Fatoman. My village is magnificent. More beautiful than Kouroussa!'

'Come off it!' I laughed. 'The railway doesn't even run near your village. Not to speak of the plane. But at Kouroussa, we have everything!'

'Oh, no you don't, Fatoman! You don't know my village. We have everything at Télimélé. Whereas at Kouroussa, last year, when I visited your mother, I saw nothing but mangrove swamps.'

'I've been told,' I said mischievously, 'that over in your little backwater an old woman once tried to make salt grow. She sowed some in her garden and watered it every day . . . Is she still in the land of the living?'

'That's a fairy tale!' she retorted, laughing.

'It's not a fairy tale, I was told about it by your own father.'

'Papa was only joking. Don't *you* ever make jokes?'

And we began to laugh and laugh . . . We were still laughing when we reached our concession.

My mother, standing at the entrance to the outer room, had no difficulty in seeing us coming. Waiting there on the threshold, one might have said she was expecting a visitor. But perhaps she was simply taking the air. And even before I had time to dismiss our bearers and to stow our luggage in a hut, the concession was invaded by our neighbors, for they had been apprised of our arrival by my mother's cries of joy. They very soon set to improvising a dance, which rapidly took on ample proportions. One after the other, the women stepped out of the huge circle of dancers to shake our hands, amid unbridled shouts of laughter.

In this way we shook innumerable hands, responded to innumerable greetings.

'Happy welcome!' they would usually shout, giving free rein to their exhilaration. 'Are your friends feeling fine? . . . Are your friends, masters and acquaintances enjoying the best of health?'

Tradition demanded that we should reply to each and every one exactly in the order of the questions asked:

'Yes, very well! All goes well over there. Our masters, our friends and acquaintances send you their greetings. They are enjoying the best of health, every single one of them.'

However, after a while we became aware that we were no longer conforming strictly to the rules of civility, because we were tired, because we had left Conakry at dawn and it was now eight in the evening.

We took our leave of the dancers as courteously as

possible, and entered my mother's hut. And our neighbors, those so-supple dancers with their ecstatic improvisations, were not long in returning to their domiciles.

My father had joined us. I can't tell, I no longer know, what state I was in at that moment. I was probably happy at being re-united with my own folks; I was sad, too, terribly stricken to see how much they had aged, how deeply marked they were by the years and by the harsh rigors of a toilsome existence. Suddenly I thought of death. But my reason told me that death is not always the consequence of old age. Bethinking myself that for the time being, and perhaps for a long time to come, I was not in a position to tender financial aid to my parents, tears suddenly drowned my eyes. Seeing the desolation on my face, they too began to weep. But certainly not for the same reasons as I did. It was my own powerlessness I was bewailing. I should have liked to have at my disposal the material means to help them enjoy their old age. But were not *they* crying for happiness? Happiness at being re-united with their son, their eldest son, grown so big and tall, and now married . . .

Marie was present at this scene, looking upset, and sitting with lowered head.

Suddenly my mother looked up and gazed at her . . .

'Daughter-in-law,' she said softly, 'is your mother enjoying the best of health?'

'Yes, mother-in-law.'

'And are your brothers and your sisters all enjoying the best of health?'

'Yes. They send you their greetings.'

'And what about you, daughter-in-law, are you enjoying the best of health?'

'I don't know, mother-in-law,' she replied sadly.

'Are you sad?'

'Oh, no,' she replied, put out.

'Aren't you glad to have come to see me?' my mother asked with a smile.

'Oh, yes! . . . of course! . . .'

'Then why are you sitting there with a face as long as a fiddle?'

Marie thought for a moment, then replied timidly:

'I wish I hadn't had to leave my mother so soon.'

'But hadn't you already left her for quite a long period?'

'Oh, yes, mother-in-law. For four years.'

'Well, then, take heart, daughter mine. Your home-sickness will pass away.'

Then, after a few minutes' silence, she added, in a motherly way:

'Take your ease. In my dwelling place you will encounter the same welcome and the same affection as you do at your mother's.'

'I do not doubt it,' cried Marie, looking happier.

My father, who was of a calmer disposition and had not taken any part in the exchange, had gone out. And my mother had already stopped crying. The sobs had ceased. As for Marie, she was once more perfectly composed. I began to question my mother:

'Did you receive my last letter?'

'Yes. But you had forgotten to say on what date you would arrive. And so we very much regret we were unable to come and meet our daughter-in-law at the station.'

'I did not tell you on purpose. I didn't want you to put yourselves out for us.'

'Do you think that would have put us out?'

'No, mother mine. But I didn't want you to overdo things! . . . I like moderation. Do you remember the days when you used to call me *Saadéni?*'*

'That's a long time ago!'

'And why did you baptise me *Saadéni?*'

*Little lamb.

'Because you loved to be alone. Do you still keep to yourself as much as ever?'

Marie, amused by the teasing way I was talking to my mother, was smiling sweetly.

'I love crowds now,' I said, to reassure my mother.

'Hey!' she cried suddenly. 'Tell me, Fatoman, did they feed you well over there?'

'Very well,' I replied.

But this answer did not seem to satisfy her, and she still seemed worried.

'Did a woman cook your meals for you?'

'A woman! No! I did it myself!'

'Did you do the cooking yourself? Like a woman?'

Marie and I burst out laughing, finding my mother's question very funny. But, on reflection, we saw that it was a reasonable question, because in all her life she had never, until now, heard of a man doing his own cooking.

'Why, yes, mother-in-law,' Marie explained with a pleasant smile, 'over there, cooking is not an art reserved exclusively for women, you know.'

'So you, daughter mine, will let your husband do his own cooking? If you don't look after him yourself, how will your children have any chance in life? You know that, according to our traditions, the future happiness of children depends upon a wife's devotion to her husband.'

'Mother-in-law, have no anxiety! Henceforward, Fatoman will not so much as set foot in a kitchen. *I* am there now.'

'Mother mine,' I broke in, 'would you have a little warm water for us? We should like to make ourselves clean.'

'Yes. The water is in the *tata*.* Go on now and bathe, then you can eat and go to bed.'

After going to the hut that had been assigned to us,

*Enclosure of plaited withies.

we took it in turn to wash off the dust of the journey. Worn out, Marie dropped off to sleep immediately. As for myself, I tried in vain to force myself to sleep. The film of my life, of the six years spent far from my native land, kept surging up from the depths of my being. Instead of sleeping, I lay with my eyes fixed on the beams and thatch of the roof, illuminated by the wan light of a storm lantern.

That night, my memories overwhelmed my mind and dimmed my sight. The film kept playing, on and on . . .

A Sleepless Night

I STILL HAD NOT reached my twentieth birthday when I left my native land for the first time.

One leaden evening, when the sun's rays were only just managing to pierce a thick mist, the plane on the regular Air France flight was circling very low over the Paris suburbs, preparing to land. Sunk in their seats, safety belts fastened, the passengers, with bated breath, were awaiting the end of their long journey from Africa.

Finally, the great metal bird had touched down; then it had trundled rather rapidly toward a horizon barred by tall houses. Afterward, losing speed, it had turned, had followed a flare path that took a turn to the right, another to the left, and had come to a halt in front of the immense buildings of Orly Airport. The passengers, conducted by hostesses, had almost immediately taken seats in a bus going to the Invalides.

That was the evening on which I experienced the cold for the first time, that horrible cold which until then I had known only through books, a purely theoretical knowledge therefore; but now, this was the real thing stinging my eyes and freezing my ears . . .

'Don't curl up! Keep moving!' had been the advice given me by a young man seated next to me who seemed alarmed when he saw me with my shoulders up to my ears under the cruel cold.

'Well, it's far from warm in here!' I had replied briefly. He did not give me any further advice.

The young man, probably a Parisian, seemed to be familiar with the region; with his face glued to the window throughout the trip, he kept murmuring the names of villages on the outskirts of Paris, names which the spasmodic roaring of the engine prevented me from hearing distinctly.

The Invalides at last! . . . Everyone started bustling around, and I got pushed about; everyone had to carry his own luggage to the waiting taxis.

It was strange, because that evening no one had come to meet me. Perhaps the cable dispatched from Africa had been delayed. But by a fortunate coincidence I had met a young African, who, I had been told at home, was studying law at Grenoble. He was called Diabaté. His nonchalant manner revealed that he was perfectly accustomed to Parisian life, to this hubbub, to these milling crowds, and above all to the cold. I had given him my name: Fatoman.

'Where are you going, Fatoman?' he asked. 'Are they expecting you in the provinces?'

'Yes, Argenteuil.'

'Argenteuil,' he declared, 'is not the provinces, but a suburb close, very close, to where we are now. You'll have no difficulty getting there. Just take the metro there, over the road.'

But he had guessed that I was having trouble following his explanations. It could be seen on my face. So he had gone on:

'Look! Go down that hole there, just over there, and follow the crowd . . . Then, at the Gare Saint-Lazare, you can catch your train for Argenteuil.'

He shook my hand, then vanished in the throng, for he told me he was in a hurry to catch the first available train to Grenoble.

After Diabaté had taken leave of me thus, I was left alone, despairingly alone, my bags and possessions scattered at random round my feet. And suddenly my thoughts had returned to the scene my mother had made the evening before, arguing with me and with my father to prevent my departure:

'Will I never have any peace of mind? . . . Yesterday it was a school in Conakry; today, it's a school in France. Tomorrow . . . who knows what it'll be tomorrow? Every day another new caper to take my son away from me! . . . Have you already forgotten how ill he was at Conakry, poor little thing?' she had added, turning on my father. 'But no, you're never content! It's sending him to France you're after now. Are you mad? Or do you want to drive *me* mad? And as for you,' she cried, wheeling upon me, 'you're nothing but a thankless child. Any excuse is good enough for you to run away from your mother. Only this time, it's not going to be as you imagine it's going to be, not by a long chalk!' And raising her eyes she had addressed the heavens: 'So many years already I've been parted from my boy!'

My thoughts continued to roam: I remembered my uncles, who had treated me in such a friendly, affectionate way; my imagination embraced the years to come, my future passions. And suddenly I felt happy, despite my loneliness . . .

And in this sunburst of happiness I thought of Diabaté, of all the fascinating things other African students from France had told me about Paris. Lifting my head, I caught sight of the Eiffel Tower and its multicolored searchlights sweeping the night sky, the Invalides with its great balloon of a dome, those monuments which everyone had told me were the most beautiful in all the world. But were beautiful monuments enough to make a city the most beautiful place in the world? This was something only the future could confirm or deny.

And I had lowered my head again; I had also caught sight of the kind of life going on all round me, a continual rumbling, composed of the thousand noises of the busy streets, the roaring of motors, the hurly-burly of the crowds, a thundering as of huge white-crested breakers . . .

Finally, I went down into the hole across the street. It was not all that difficult. I realized that the 'jaws of the underground,' where the crowds were thickest, must lead further on and be connected somehow with the platform of this dazzlingly lighted tunnel. Until then, I had never imagined that such a tunnel could exist there at the heart of the city. It must certainly have been there a long time. I had simply reflected that, without this opening, this deep tunnel, I would not have been able to hear the echoes of the trains' rumblings and whistlings which had suddenly struck my ears.

I say: 'Which had suddenly struck my ears,' for after that everything had become calm; so calm that I was beginning to have some doubts about where the tunnel would lead me, and to feel somewhat worried about the directions given me by Diabaté regarding this tunnel. I was really wondering whether I should go on; already I was thinking of retracing my steps. But then I had been surprised by the sound of footsteps behind me: a man was whistling in a carefree manner. He seemed so sure of himself and so full of go that the sight of him filled me with fresh courage and self-confidence. So I kept on. The man was wearing a faded brown cap whose peak shadowed a low, narrow forehead; despite the cold, he was sweating, and panting, as if he had just finished some peculiarly exhausting task.

'You going to catch the metro, too?' he asked me.

I was carrying my suitcases in either hand. Seizing the heavier of the two, the one holding my books, in less than no time he had tied a broad leather strap around it and hoisted it on his shoulder; then, striding on ahead of me, he moved off in the direction of the platform.

'I'm going to Saint-Lazare,' I said. 'Thank you for helping me.'

'I see you don't know your way around these parts.'

I was glad that this man was giving me a hand, but his help seemed so unexpected that already I was feeling some doubts about my companion's morality.

A *colon* had told me, on the eve of my departure: 'You'll be encountering these men on their own wandering almost everywhere in the big cities; you ought to beware of them; they're up to no good.'

And now here I was ignoring his warning; I had accepted the companionship of this stranger, who was now striding along in front of me with my suitcase on his broad shoulders. All the same, I felt some hesitation about asking him to give it back to me.

'Oh yes,' he was saying, 'I'm not afraid to roll my sleeves up, specially at night. One sleeps better with one's sleeves rolled up.'

What did he mean? Was he pulling my leg? I don't like to be taken for someone more stupid and more naïve than I really am. I know perfectly well that one works better, that one is better able to carry a load with one's sleeves rolled up; but it was the first time I had heard that one sleeps better with the cloth of one's sleeves bundled up above the elbow.

The man must surely have been fighting with someone, I thought; and he must have gone at it hammer-and-tongs, judging by the sweat pouring down his forehead. Had it been a gangster's quarrel? Were they not disquieting, that energy, and that apparent serenity of his features, after such a brawl? It was disquieting, as if he had been about to strike me myself, as if he had really been going to do me in.

'Where were you coming from, when I first saw you?' I asked him in a voice that was not very steady.

'From the Halles. I work at the Halles.'

I did not then know what that meant. And because I did not understand him completely, I was suddenly overcome by a fresh wave of fear. Nevertheless, to run away was out of the question, without running the risk of appearing ridiculous in the eyes of all those passengers streaming through the tunnel. That was why, before venturing any further with this man, I so much wanted to know more about him, to find out whether, far from the passing throng, so reassuring in its normality, it might not enter his head to attack and rob me.

'What is your name, monsieur?' I inquired, in a voice choking with fear.

But obviously he had no idea that I was suspicious of him, for he replied at once, in a confident manner:

'Stanislas.'

We went on walking. And then we reached the platform. The electric lights cast their crude illumination on the ground, and were reflected even more clearly on the tiled vaulting of the metro station's roof. Stanislas was standing beside me on the platform; he appeared to be a reliable person. But might he not just be pretending to be so? 'He's a brute, a real brute!' I thought to myself. But my reason told me: 'No, there's no real brutality about him. It must be something else, something quite cold and calculating, a well-concealed aggressiveness. Surely he must have seized my suitcase with the intention of stealing it? He must certainly be hiding things from me; under that low, narrow fore-

head many secret thoughts must be hidden. Even when
one's forehead is broad and high, quite a lot of evil
thoughts can lurk behind its apparently noble façade . . .'

I remembered the *colon's* advice: 'You'll be encountering these men on their own wandering almost everywhere in the big cities; you ought to beware of
them; they're up to no good . . .'

This advice, flashing through my memory once
again, had undermined my assurance: I felt extremely
uncomfortable now.

'Stanislas is a sly one; he inspires disgust rather than
fear,' I said to myself again. I no longer felt any fear,
but an incommensurable disgust . . . We stood waiting
for a while, and then finally, with a great metallic
clatter, the train entered the station. When it stopped,
Stanislas opened a door and we both hastily entered the
carriage. Almost at once the train shot off again, the
doors closing automatically with a hiss.

'Off again already?' I thought. 'The trains over here
don't stay as long at a station as they do in Africa. No
sooner arrived than they're off.'

Our carriage was packed to suffocation. Lovers,
standing facing one another, were whispering tender
nothings in one another's ears, without paying heed to
anyone. The people who were seated were mostly old
folk, reading their newspapers with an air of indiffer-
ence. No one seemed to bother about anyone else;
everyone minded his own business.

The train rumbled and rattled on and on . . . At
some points, it rocked and swayed. We changed to
another line . . . Finally, a vast hall, then Saint-Lazare,
where a multitude of trains stood waiting for their
passengers under an immense vaulted roof.

Stanislas, pointing out the train to Argenteuil, told
me to take a seat in a third-class compartment.

Heaving a deep sigh, I thanked him.

'Good-bye,' he replied in an affectionate tone of voice, as if he had been addressing a younger brother.

I gave him a closer look. I couldn't believe my eyes. Had the *colon's* advice been wrong, or was it simply that it did not apply to Stanislas? Yet Stanislas was a man wandering about alone, walking all alone in the corridors of the metro . . . My head buzzed with contradictions. Despite myself, I began confessing *mea culpa*; I revealed to the man the apprehensions that had been agitating my breast.

'Thank you again, and with all my heart, Monsieur Stanislas. Perhaps this is the moment to tell you that I was very frightened . . .'

He stared at me in surprise, as if he had been struck by a thunderbolt.

'Frightened of what?' he demanded.

'Of you.'

'What on earth did you think?'

'I had heard so much about this city, about the men on their own who wander around Paris, that I didn't feel at all happy all the time we were traveling in the metro. Yet there was nothing in your behavior that should have caused me any anxiety.'

He looked me straight in the eyes. Obviously he had understood more than I had said, and perhaps he had even guessed the attitude of mind of certain African *colons*, for he growled in reply:

'Yes, I've got it! The *colons* look upon your lot as cannibalistic Negroes. At least, that's what they say over here. To those same men, we Frenchmen are nothing but brigands, isn't that it? That's what they tell you over there, isn't it?'

'But monsieur . . .'

He interrupted me. And I realized that I should not be able to say another word until he had got it off his chest, got it all off his chest:

'Only I don't fall for that line!' he cried. 'During the

war, my best friend was a Senegalese. An intelligent
man, just as intelligent as us. Oh, yes, I know the tune
the *colons* play, that dreary little tune, I know what it
is! What are you all waiting for? Why don't you just
boot them all into the sea?'

I was confused, but I managed to stammer out a few
more words of cordial thanks, for now the train was
beginning to move.

'I don't fall for that line!' Stanislas repeated. 'Boot
the lot of them into the sea, they're only exploiting you
and oppressing you!'

Those were the words I caught through the noise of
the wind as the train gathered speed . . .

I kept waving to him right up to the moment when
we lost sight of one another. When I sat down, I said
to myself: that man is a brother to all men. Would
the rest of the French people be as brotherly? Only
time, the many years I was to spend in that country,
could reveal that to me.

Now the train was arriving in the station at Argenteuil. A man whose acquaintance I had made was
walking with me down a street. He was called Pierre
and hailed from Marseilles. It was fairly light, that
night. The electric street lamps shed sufficient illumination to rid even the most cowardly of men of any sense
of fear. In fact, we were walking in a light even
brighter than the light of the moon. I was preoccupied
by the weight of my suitcases, by my feet which had
been made excessively sensitive by the rigor of the cold
and the hard pavements.

'You'd better get a move on,' the man said. 'I have to
get home, where some friends are awaiting me.'

But it was difficult for me to walk any faster; besides, a violent, icy wind was blowing and whipping my
ears which heard very little of what he was saying.

'Yes,' I gasped. 'I'm coming.'

'I believe I've lost the way,' he muttered. 'But we'll

make inquiries at the police station, not far from here.'

We were still moving slowly. Now I was fairly accustomed to carrying my heavy suitcases, to battling along through the cold, even though my hands and my ears felt as stiff and dry as dead leaves. The thought of soon being able to get out of the glacial wind and take refuge in a warm room, a room heated to African temperature, gave me renewed courage, and already seemed to be warming my heart and my frozen limbs.

In front of the police station a police officer was leaning against a police van opposite the entrance.

'I've got a Negro here who arrived at Orly by the eight o'clock plane,' Pierre explained.

Pierre thought a bit, seeming embarrassed, then added:

'A black, I should say. Excuse me. I don't know—we don't know, over here, if we should say Negro or black.'

The policeman was watching us, and me in particular, with an inquiring air, as if I were some victim he had before him and from whom he had to extort a full confession by the fixity of his gaze.

'Call me what you like,' I replied. 'Negro or black. The main thing is that I arrived by plane from Africa this evening and that I'd like to get to my school here in Argenteuil as soon as possible.'

I handed the policeman an envelope bearing the address to which I had to go.

The policeman had been looking me straight in the face while I was speaking, and the doubtful expression that had appeared on his face had disappeared. Now confidence instead of doubt glowed on his features.

'You speak French jolly well!' Pierre cried, in sudden surprise.

Then, going up to the van, he added:

'He says he arrived this evening from Africa, that he has never lived in France and yet he speaks absolutely correct French!'

'But they are the same as us!' the policeman retorted. 'They are French like us. We built schools and hospitals out there. In a few years, they'll be just like us. They'll have their own regiments and everything.'

He opened the door of the van and invited me to take a seat.

'Good-bye, Monsieur Pierre,' I called, as the van was moving off.

'Good-bye!' he called back.

'You're not exactly warmly dressed,' the policeman commented, giving me a look. 'It begins to get cold at this time of the year.'

'It *begins* to get cold, you say? I'm already perished!'

'Oh, this is nothing, nothing to speak about! Soon there'll be frost, and then snow. It's lovely, the snow!'

'Snow!' I cried.

'Yes, and there'll be fog. And sometimes the temperature even descends below zero.'

The black van, which the policeman affectionately called his Black Maria, had driven down several rather unsavory looking narrow streets before regaining the main road, which was bordered by strictly identical houses. I was finally set down outside a yard swarming with students; this was where, during the next few years, I was to be given a practical and theoretical training destined to make of me a good motor mechanic.

At the end of the year, I left the technical school with my diploma, and at the same time succeeded in passing the entrance examination for an institution of higher learning. But then, totally unexpectedly, my country's Territorial Assembly chose that moment to cut off the grant which had been allotted to me. This was done

without any reference to my proved ability, on the
pretext that the diploma I had obtained was sufficient
qualification for my future career.

My life as a boarder had been comfortable at the
school in Argenteuil, where I had lived with young
Frenchmen without suffering (or, it would be fairer to
say, without even feeling) any kind of racial discrimi-
nation. When I left the school to pursue further studies
in Paris proper, my difficulties began, difficulties of all
kinds. Need I enumerate them? Lack of money to pay,
first of all, my tuition fees, and secondly, the rent of a
tiny room on the sixth floor of a block in the Rue
Lamartine; thirdly, the cost of food and clothing and
the articles needed for my student life. All these demands—to me, enormous—had to be met if I wanted
to realize my ambitions! . . . Until then, alas, I had
lived, as my readers may well suppose, at the expense
of the Colony, thanks to the Colonial Government! . . .
I very soon realized that my dreams and my ambitions
—however talented I might be—were not enough to
live on.

In the society in which I found myself, an ultra-
modern society in which everything is based on capital,
if ambition and intelligence are not backed up by capital they slowly fritter away and finally turn to dust and
ashes. This is easily understandable: the majority of
teaching establishments for higher education are the
fruit of private initiative; in order to follow the lectures
at such places, the students must pay tuition fees,
which form an important contribution to the upkeep of
these establishments.

'During the first term, I shall work hard in class,' I
told myself. 'I shall send my report card to the Colony.
And my high marks will persuade the Scholarship
Committee to reverse its decision on my case.'

I put this plan into action. Three months went by,
during which I really put my shoulder to the wheel.

Three months of hard labor, three months of starvation, three months of unpaid rent! But my report card, sent to the Territorial Assembly's Scholarship Committee, accompanied by an enthusiastic letter of recommendation from the Director of the teaching establishment, remained without reply. And several of my African comrades were victims of the same incomprehensible bureaucratic inertia.

'My dear child, you may continue with your studies,' said the Director. 'We can wait and see what happens . . . Within the next year they will surely come to recognize your ability and send help from your country.'

But would the school's generously patient attitude, which for the time being assured me exemption from tuition fees, prove sufficient to allow me to finish the course? As I have already said, there were the hotel expenses to be paid, and the manager of that particular establishment in the Rue Lamartine was a far from patient man. And the cost of food . . . As for transportation costs, that was unthinkable; transport was dispensable: my feet would take the place of taxis, buses and the metro.

One evening, the hotel manager said to me:

'Monsieur, you still haven't settled your rent for this term.'

'Please wait a little longer. I still haven't received any reply from my country.'

'If your parents know they can't support you,' he grumbled, 'why do they send you to France?'

I could find no answer to that. Words would have been useless. It was his rent he wanted.

On the other hand, I could not tell him that I was not being supported by my parents. He had elevated them to a position to which they could not possibly aspire, that of being able to pay the costs of educating one of their sons in France! . . . I did not want to tell him that as long as my country remained an underdeveloped nation, Guinean families would not be rich enough to pay the expenses of educating their children in France. I could not remonstrate with this man in any way. He was my creditor. What he wanted from me was his money. Moreover, as soon as he heard the rustle of notes, he became as obliging as possible, and gentle as a lamb. But if one of his tenants was without funds, the manager turned gloomy and insolent and never so much as gave him the time of day.

'Until we meet again, monsieur,' I said, taking leave of him.

He did not reply. I heard him shouting after me, as I went toward the door:

'You've got to pay this evening, d'you hear? This evening without fail. I want to keep my books straight. I've had enough of you! If all my tenants were like you, how could I run a hotel like this? How would we pay our taxes and meet all the other outlays?'

I shut the door on him. At that moment, I felt as though a thunderbolt had dropped on my head. Where was I to find by that evening the necessary funds to pay my rent, to have some peace of mind again? . . . I had eaten nothing since the night before. All morning I'd had nothing in my belly but water. What was I to do? . . . 'Yes, what *am* I to do?' I kept asking myself. And then I understood why, in the streets of that city, there were men and women walking about alone, talking to themselves or gesticulating, crushed by eternal material problems, haunted by the specter of insufficient money, because always it is the sly and evil ones who get their claws on money, leaving only the smallest trifle for the rest of the people.

I had walked along the boulevard to the Quartier Latin. I wanted to see Mme Aline, an old lady of seventy summers hailing from Normandy, who lived in the Rue Saint-Jacques and who was the mother of all young Africans. (It was they who had nicknamed her

"Tante Aline," Aunt Aline.) The shop windows were crammed with delicious things to eat . . . Sometimes the shopgirls would draw me like magnets, as they offered to sell me their wares. Though I hadn't a penny in my pocket, I feasted my eyes on the displays, so that I would often walk for miles and miles, without realizing it, my eyes on the windows. There were many others like me, gazing into the windows; lovers, arm in arm, strolled nonchalantly along.

'Ah, there you are Fatoman,' Aunt Aline greeted me as soon as she saw me enter the Bar de Capoulade.

'Yes. I'm thankful to find you here.'

'Sit down beside me,' she said, indicating a chair.

Then she just looked at me and understood, without my saying a word, that hunger was gnawing at my vitals.

'Order whatever you like. It's on me,' she said.

'No,' I said. 'I'm not hungry. I had something to eat and drink not long ago.'

She looked at me again. My strained face belied what I had said.

'Come on, don't be embarrassed!' she cried. 'Your friend Lamine told me this morning that your grant had been stopped and that you haven't a brass farthing. Look, Fatoman! . . . Between friends, let me tell you you're hungry, you've gone hungry for more than one day. You haven't eaten anything for at least thirty-six hours.'

'That's true,' I admitted in a low voice.

'I knew it. At my age—I'm seventy you know—one knows everything, or almost everything. But if you're hungry and won't tell your best friend about it, if you're afraid of losing face, you'll finish up by dying of starvation in this country. D'you understand?'

'Yes. But I'm not going to proclaim my hunger from the rooftops.'

'You're standing on your dignity! Such dignity is out

of place. If you don't tell your friends you are hungry, they will never realize it.'

'I'm not hiding anything from you,' I said in a low voice, eating the sandwich that the waiter had just put before me.

'And you do well to do so, my son. It's in your own interests. Later, much later, when you've gone back to your country, you'll forget it all. Because when you get back there your efforts will have been crowned with success,' she added, giving a gay laugh, as if trying to make me forget my present miseries.

'And do you really think it'll be like that, Aunt Aline?' I asked.

'Yes. Of course it will. You can be sure of that!' she assured me, giving a smile that displayed healthy teeth of a surprising whiteness in a lady of her advanced age.

'Suffering is something one gets over,' I said. 'But what one never gets over is the fact of having suffered; that always leaves its mark on a man, on his inmost heart, unless he retains the adaptability of a little child.'

'Perhaps. But sufferings like these are nothing!' she declared gaily. 'Did you receive any reply to your request for a grant?'

'They still haven't answered.'

'In that case, Fatoman, wouldn't it be wiser not to persist in your studies? With the references you have, you are now a technician capable of finding work in any kind of factory.'

'That's an excellent idea,' I said. 'I'll take your advice.'

'If you work in a factory, you can attend evening classes. Then later on you can see how things work out.'

She took out of her handbag a little bundle of bank-

notes which she passed to me under the table, so that
no one would see.

'How good you are to me!' I sighed.

'*Au revoir* and good luck,' she replied, shaking me
by the hand. 'I'm the mother of all the Africans. All
those who return to Africa will remember me. The
number of Africans I've helped! And I shall go on
helping them till the end of my days. Did you know I
could speak Malinké?'

'No!'

'For a long period I lived at Siguiri. I left there in
1925.'

'I was still not born then, Aunt Aline.'

'We'll talk about that some other time. Now, son, be
off with you,' she concluded with a burst of laughter.
'By the way, my granddaughter, Françoise, has promised to go and visit you. She too is very fond of Africans.'

'*Au revoir*, and thank you again,' I called to her as I
went through the bar door. 'I shall be delighted to see
Françoise again.'

I went back down the Boulevard Saint-Michel. I
wanted to go back to the hotel; but remembering that
the manager was there and that he would ask for the
money I owed him, I changed my mind, turned round
like an automaton and went along the Boulevard Saint-
Germain. Along this boulevard, just before reaching
Saint-Germain-des-Prés, there was a a small bar called
La Pergola; and as the menu there was not very dear, I
went in. All the customers were young and destitute
inhabitants of the Quartier Latin, both white and
black. And because we were all in the same boat, a
staunch camaraderie existed between us all. We used to
dance and sing. The girls had short hair, wore trousers
and dark sweaters, and smoked like men.

From time to time, old men came in. What could
they be wanting in that place? One of them, coming up

to me, spoke to me in terms I did not understand. He sat down next to me, and soon he began to make advances to me, advances as bold as those which perhaps a young man makes to a young girl.

'What are you up to?' I cried, scandalized. 'Is this man mad? . . . Can't you see what he's doing?'

'What?' said Liliane, who was seated on my right.

'This old man! He's stroking my thighs! What does he take me for?'

Liliane burst out laughing, then signed:

'My! You're really frightened, aren't you! . . . Don't you know he's a queer?'

And she then gave me a lengthy explanation about what that word meant.

'Oh, no!' I protested. 'There's nothing like that goes on in my country. Out there, a man is made to live with a woman. A man is supposed to marry in order to produce children.'

'You'll never get the hang of things here!' she said. 'We all have our vices over here! You Africans are pure. You know nothing about our tricks and perversions. So much the better, too.'

'Whether I ever get the hang of you or not!' I replied in a voice choking with disgust, 'I shall never set foot again in this bar. Never, d'you hear me? . . . Never. Good-bye.'

I rushed out, sickened by this new thing I had discovered, this sordid thing. I had not shaken hands with my comrades, those comrades who probably would spend all night there getting drunk. The majority of them, in fact, had no home, could not afford the luxury of even an uncomfortable hotel room and so did not know where to sleep except in that bar. As I left, as I was taking leave of them, some, sprawled in their seats, had already closed their eyes . . .

It was fairly late, but people were still wandering about the streets. Paris was not asleep yet. It is a city

that is never completely asleep. But probably the hotel
manager had now gone to sleep. He usually went to
bed after midnight. I had been walking for some time;
already I had crossed the Jardin du Louvre and
reached the Avenue de l'Opéra. Dark thoughts were
passing through my mind: I recalled that old man who
just now had tried to arouse me sexually in La Pergola,
that crazy creature who had felt my leg. Suddenly I
remembered the advice of the *colon* in Conakry:

'Beware of those men on their own whom you'll
encounter wandering almost everywhere in the big
cities!'

My reason countered with:

'That man who stroked my leg was not one of those.
The thing happened right in a crowded bar.'

Distraught, I walked on through the night, obsessed
by that old man and by the thought of my hotel manager, who was getting impossible to deal with. As I
approached my lodgings, my heart began to beat very
fast, as it did every night on my return. Out of fear, I
removed my shoes and walked in my bare feet on the
cold pavement. But I did not feel the cold, I only felt
an anguished fear. I pressed the button that automatically opened the door. I was very afraid that it would
squeak. But it made no noise. I cast a quick look round
the entrance hall; all the main lights were off. There
was only a small lamp at the end of the hall, shedding
a reddish light. But I was still afraid that the manager
might have concealed himself somewhere in the shadows, ready to jump out on me. Openmouthed, hardly
daring to breathe, I moved forward on tiptoe. I
climbed the stairs, four steps at a time, my heart beating fit to burst. Quietly, I pushed open the door of my
room, and, heaving a deep sigh, flung myself on the
bed.

When, having recovered from my terrors, I was able
to get up again, I discovered, on lighting my bedside

lamp, that my possessions and my suitcases, stowed away in the wardrobe, had vanished . . .

In despair, I was just about to call the police to investigate the robbery when I saw, on the bedside table, a little note. Had Françoise called to see me while I was wandering about the Quartier Latin? . . . Alas, it was not her writing! It was the manager's writing. The note was couched in the following terms:

'When you have paid your rent, the hotel desk will return your property.'

Worried, I sat down again on the bed. There was nothing left in my room: all my possessions had been taken away. From now on, everything would become the property of the manager until I had paid my debt. Yes, even the battered saucepans I had used to cook in, to prepare that peanut sauce which brought back to mind so vividly my mother's style of cooking.

'That manager's pretty cunning!' I thought. Alarmed by my lowliness, by my poverty, he had been afraid that I might take flight. So he had seized my things in order to intimidate me.

'That manager's no fool. He's very astute!'

Then, talking to myself in a low, a very low voice, I told myself: 'Tomorrow, I must find work.'

To this, an inner voice replied:

'If you had gone back to Africa, as the government of the Colony requested you to do, you would now be leading a happy life there.'

'No, no!' I cried aloud. 'I shan't go back. I shall carry on my studies, whatever it costs, to prove to myself that I can do even better.'

And the inner voice kept replying, untiringly, inexorably:

'In this country, in order to do what you want to do, you must have the means to do it, that is, you must have money. And you have absolutely nothing at all! Already the manager has collected the few little posses-

sions that stood between you and dire poverty, that
protected your lowliness. You should have replied to
the offers of jobs in your native land.'

Then:

'No, no, I *won't* go back!' I kept repeating this one
phrase, as if obsessed, as if to compel my reason to
keep quiet and stop making any further reproaches.
But can the reason be silenced? Can an upright mind
remain dumb?

I lay down. It was two o'clock in the morning. I
knew that the hotel manager would get up at six
o'clock. There was nothing to do but catch a little
sleep, take some rest; then wake up and quietly leave
the hotel, very early, before he awoke ...

Three months went by, and my life was nothing but
poverty and destitution, complete destitution. Yes,
three months of hide-and-seek with the hotel manager,
three months of vain seeking for work, three months of
famine! ... Things were so bad that, one afternoon, in
the depths of despair and having spent some time at
the Odéon crossing watching a sword-swallower to try
to forget my miseries, I had hardly taken a few steps in
the direction of the École de Médecine when I suddenly half lost consciousness. I shivered; my brain
seemed to grow dull and opaque. Nevertheless I forced
myself on toward the Capoulade bar, in the hope of
finding Aunt Aline there. But it was useless trying to
walk: hunger clouded my eyes and my trembling legs
refused to obey me. Yet now I was accustomed to
starvation. It often happened that I spent a whole day,
and even two days without putting anything in my
stomach apart from water, coffee or tea. And it didn't
bother me, it didn't seem to bother me any more.
Sometimes, I didn't even remember that I had not
eaten. My stomach, as if shrunken, really shrunken
through lack of food, no longer felt hunger.

But that afternoon—was I suddenly going mad?

For a moment I was clinging to one of the École de Médecine's gray walls; and as I tried to recollect, to think, to wonder what to do, it seemed to me that my brain was half dead or was refusing to function at all. Then I wanted desperately to get away from that street packed with students and take refuge in a bar; but I couldn't do a thing. I collapsed on the pavement . . . I got up again with difficulty, and again clung to the wall. The passers-by appeared now wavering now double, exactly as if I were losing my sight . . .

Gradually recovering consciousness a little after that attack of near-madness, I reckoned, counting on my fingers, that it was three days since I had eaten anything. Three days during which I hadn't had a cent in my pockets.

'Three days of hunger! It's the first time that's happened,' I murmured. 'If I don't want to die here like a dog, I must find work, and find it today! I simply must!'

I stumbled on. Perhaps I should find Aunt Aline at the Capoulade. She was usually there at the end of the afternoons. I lifted my head and gazed into the distance, in the direction of the tables on the terrace outside the bar. But there were no chairs outside, it was too cold. I hastened my steps, afraid that Aunt Aline might leave the Capoulade before I had seen her.

'There she is! . . . I can see her! . . . She's there!' I shouted, like a madman.

'Good afternoon, Aunt Aline! Things aren't going too well,' I said timidly, sitting down beside her.

'What, Fatoman, still no work?'

She looked at me with a pitiful expression on her face. 'How thin you've become!' she cried.

'Yes,' I replied. 'Things aren't going well at all.'

We remained silent for a while. And I could hear the

voice, still the same voice, whispering in my ear: 'If you had gone back to your native land when they asked you to, you wouldn't have all these troubles.'

Suddenly my eyes flooded with tears. I wiped them away rapidly and discreetly, for I did not want Aunt Aline to see the deep distress in my soul. But lifting her head, she said to me slowly, stressing each word:

'I understand! I can tell from the look on your face that things are not going well with you. I've been wanting to see you for days . . . about work at the Halles. Students go there every night.'

'Where is it?' I asked eagerly.

'Not far from here. Beyond the Châtelet, on the Boulevard Sébastopol.'

'Ah, yes, I see!'

'You can earn a thousand francs every night.'

'Has one to work all through the night?'

'No. You have to unload trucks, for three hours . . . It's not very pleasant, unloading trucks at night, especially during this terribly cold weather. But it's better than nothing!'

'I'll go there tonight.'

'Good luck,' she said, quietly slipping a few bank-notes into my hand.

'You're so good to me. May God preserve our friendship!'

'I hope so too, my son. Good luck for tonight.'

Every night at ten o'clock, trucks coming from distant provinces would arrive and pull up in the district round Les Halles. They brought food supplies for the populace of Paris and the inner suburbs. Every night it was the same thing, the same procession of trucks arriving, trucks which the porters at the Halles called 'routiers.'

We worked in teams. Some, on top of the trucks, had the job of heaving the heavy sacks of foodstuffs to the next men, who carried them a few steps to others;

these would untie the packages and arrange the produce in suitable order.

I belonged to the porters' group, and now I readily understood why Stanislas, my guide in the metro, the companion of my first hour in Paris, he of whom I had been so afraid, had rolled up his sleeves. I understood why his jacket was worn and torn; I also understood why his forehead was low and narrow. Because work at the Halles was extremely hard and brutish, even for those accustomed to it, those who had bulging muscles; and even more so for us, who had come not out of love for the task, but to put a few banknotes into our permanently empty pockets.

It was cold, terribly cold, and the wet ground was strewn with slimy rubbish that made our feet slither and slip. If one didn't take care, one was likely to find oneself sprawled on the ground with a broken leg or arm.

'When will all classes of society be equal?' I would often cry in my distress. 'Can it be right for some, a minority, to be millionaires or billionaires, while we, the majority, are stupidly dying of hunger? While we have to stoop and humiliate ourselves to get a bite to eat?'

Work at the Halles was indeed humiliating. One encountered there all those who had become embittered with life, and who consequently did not use very choice terms in their speech; fellows so bruised by life that after working all night they would go and get drunk early in the morning with the fruits of their labors, or else squander it foolishly playing at cards.

'A society like this is a drug,' I thought. 'When money falls into your hands, you forget everything in order to treat yourself to one of the delusive pleasures offered by western civilization. But when there's no money, one could live one's whole life in Paris without suspecting the existence of so many delusive joys, or that this city is one of the most beautiful in the world; and then life becomes as difficult, lonely and hostile as in a desert.'

A man who has not known poverty in Paris cannot imagine the disturbance of mind, the distress and disequilibrium of spirit into which even the most hardened souls are plunged by the sense of powerlessness attendant upon lack of money.

Those few weeks I spent working at the Halles before finding regular employment changed my existence. Now I was eating every day. The one shirt I had to my back (and whose collar was always dirty, for the hotel manager still held my things) was supplemented by a new one. My shoes, their soles worn out by six months of ceaseless tramping around Paris, gave way to a new pair. And I realized that I was no longer a sort of outcast; strange to relate, an inner transformation had taken place, though I had not realized it. Those preliminary trials during my life in the western world had made of me a human being who was satified with very little. I had become simple. And from then on, in everything I did, even at meals, I would find myself cutting out everything that was not indispensable.

One fine spring morning, I went for an interview at the Simca factory in Nanterre and by chance I was taken on. I started work at once.

That evening, on my return, I pulled myself together and summoned up enough courage to go and see the hotel manager.

'Would you have the goodness,' I asked him in a dignified manner, 'to restore my effects to me. I have finally started to work. Your rent will now be paid. Little by little, of course. I can offer you these guarantees.'

With great self-assurance I drew from my pocket my driving license and my passport and laid them before him on his desk. Then I showed him my work permit,

the work permit from the Simca factory. At once the
smile re-appeared on that hard businessman's face, a
smile which only the prospect of making money could
bring into being.

'With your high qualifications,' he said happily,
'you'll certainly be able to make a lot of money at that
place.'

I looked him straight in the eyes. I felt like telling
him that a man should not be valued according to what
he has in the bank or the amount of his monthly sal-
ary, that a human being is worth more than all the
bank accounts on earth. But I should never have been
able to convince him, for I knew by painful experience
that our ideas on this subject were different and indeed
diametrically opposed. And as I wanted my things returned to me, I controlled myself and remained silent.

'I certainly hope so,' I said.

My possessions were returned to me immediately.
My one wish was to see Aunt Aline again; I also
wanted to meet her granddaughter Françoise again, for
Françoise was my 'guardian.' I went off to the Capoulade and found them there. But a few minutes later,
Aunt Aline took leave of us, saying she was in a hurry
to attend a meeting. Her young granddaughter Françoise kept me company.

'Now, Fatoman,' she said, after making sure her
grandmother had gone and that no one was listening,
'now we can get married.'

'Why? . . . Your grandmother has been preaching
the virtues of pure friendship, which gives us an un-
adulterated happiness. And she is so good to me, she
has helped me so much, that I couldn't have an easy
conscience if I were to deceive her. Aren't we all right,
just as we are, just good friends?'

'Yes, Fatoman, we are,' she said. 'But we must legal-
ize our friendship, we must get married.'

'In our hearts, everything is legal. I believe that's the

essential thing. And besides, Françoise, what if I have
a girl friend out there whom I have loved for years
before ever knowing you?'

She started. Anger made the blood rush to her
face.

'So you prefer the girls from your own country?
They're better built than we are, aren't they?' she
said.

'That's not the question,' I answered.

'You must choose, Fatoman. You can't love two
girls at once.'

'Yes, of course. Would you give me a little time to
think about it? You'll understand, later on. Now it's
time for me to see you back home, otherwise you may
be scolded by Aunt Aline on your return.'

We left the Capoulade. It was a fine day; the beginning of spring had brought the whole of Paris out of
doors, and everyone was taking a stroll. The people
were sauntering happily along the boulevards and the
streets. The café terraces were packed with customers.
All hearts were bursting with happiness; the very sky
was radiant with joy. In the Rue Soufflot, the girl students, mostly elegant and svelte, because they had put
on diaphanous dresses that molded their forms, seemed
even more lovely than usual, more bewitching than in
winter. And whenever the breeze lifted the flounces of
a dress a little, the male students, delighted, would turn
round, their hearts aflame, and call out their appreciation of the beautiful legs thus revealed. The owners of
the legs accepted the pleasantries with a smile.

And I thought to myself that no matter where we
are it is the same thing: there are girls like these who
very often keep us on tenterhooks, who often themselves suffer silently because of us, whom we are
sometimes unfaithful to, but to whom we cannot be
indifferent: they are a necessary evil, indispensable, and
without them life would be devoid of meaning.

As we walked along the Rue Saint-Jacques, Françoise, suddenly attacked by jealousy, murmured sadly:

'Why do you keep looking at the girls? Are they more beautiful than me?'

'You're an angel, Françoise,' I told her. 'But they too are beautiful. I cannot remain indifferent to my native land.'

'What native land?' she grumbled. 'You're going out of your mind, I'm sure! We're talking about girls, not about your native land.'

'Yes, that's what I mean: I've two native lands in this world—Africa and beauty. All beautiful things please me so much that I desire to possess them. Yes, even these fays, whom I often yearn to possess, but who never give me so much as a look! It's quite true that one only loves things that hurt one, things which, like women, turn rebels in our arms, refuse to let themselves be dominated.'

'Oh!' she protested. 'And what about you? . . . Do you think you'd allow yourself to be tamed for a single second?'

'Of course! But not by you. Aunt Aline asked us both to think of each other as brother and sister.'

'If she still thinks that way, I'm going to have a word with grandmother right now. I'll have a thing or two to tell her, you may be sure!'

'Now don't go creating a scandal, Françoise, I beg of you.'

'*Au revoir*, Fatoman. See you Sunday,' she said suddenly.

She gave me a peck on the cheek.

'*Au revoir*, my sister. Don't forget to give Aunt Aline a kiss from me. Tell her that I'll be paying you a visit soon.'

She did not reply. She went away, walking rapidly along the Rue Saint-Jacques. I stayed where I was, waiting until the crowd of students, both girls and boys, should have hidden her from my sight. And because she knew I was following her with my eyes, she took care to swing her hips as she walked, and this touched my heart. I was already about to call her back, to tell her she was beautiful, that I didn't want her to go away, that I wanted to have her always beside me, when the press of passers-by hid her from my sight . . .

I strolled quietly back to my hotel, read a little, then went to bed.

The next morning, the usual daily routine of work started again.

And every morning, there were the same metro stations, the same crowds hounded by the necessity of making a living, the same buses to Nanterre. And every night, after supper, the same enthralling books. Often I would fall asleep with my mind hundreds of leagues from Paris, carried away and rocked to sleep by extraordinary romantic adventures. I had soon built a life for myself, my own way of living, seeking no company but that of Françoise and Aunt Aline.

Every morning, without fail, the same work started again at the Simca factory, that factory that resembled a real virgin forest; a forest with mysterious rumblings, with great stretches of green and innumerable lianas. From six in the morning, this great forest of metal would begin to hum. There was nothing to be heard but hammerings and squealings; and in the evening, in the open spaces behind the factory, we all, the authors of those squealings and hammerings, would go to contemplate the fruits of our labor. Hundreds of cars were lined up there: cars which were far beyond the resources of our wallets.

I invariably went to Aunt Aline's one evening in three.

Later on, when winter came back and Paris was filled with people again, my life began to know new pleasures; after Françoise's lectures were over, we would take walks along the Seine, along the quays, in the gardens of the Louvre and the Luxembourg. I often went to concerts, to the Opéra and the Comédie-Française. Aunt Aline and Françoise did all they could to make me like classical music, for which they had a passion, but which repelled me. In the end, I only came to like it because of their perseverance.

Then it was Christmas.

On Christmas Day, Aunt Aline and Françoise, hoping to make me forget the rigors of daily life and of winter, took me to the finest cabaret in Paris. That evening's outing temporarily reconciled me to the gray skies and the gray houses of Paris. The Parisians were singing and celebrating their *Noël*. Everywhere in the city the windows of the big shops blazed with multi-colored, scintillating lights. Often, the mysterious birth of Christ was pictured there.

In the nightclub happiness knew no bounds. It burst forth in the heavens and in all our hearts. That evening, we all seemed to have come from the same father and mother. We all addressed one another as friends. It was Christmas, wasn't it?

That festivity was for me a great joy whose memory I shall cherish for many years to come.

But a few days later I found myself in the hospital. Lying in bed, I kept on lamenting:

'If only my father were here!' My voice was sad.

'I am here, beside you,' Françoise would say. 'Don't worry, Fatoman. You'll get better soon.'

When the woman doctor entered the room, Aunt Aline cried:

'Doctor, help us! Help us! This boy must get well. He has no one belonging to him over here . . .'

'Madame,' the doctor had replied in a reassuring tone, 'do not excite yourself. You can be quite sure we shall give him the most careful attention.'

In that woman there was something very human,

and she had a great confidence in her ability as a doctor. When Aunt Aline and Françoise followed her out into the corridor, she told them:

'Your friend has caught a pulmonary infection. We shall have to operate on him.'

'Do whatever you can, doctor,' sighed Aunt Aline in a supplicating voice. 'Do everything you can to bring him back to health and strength.'

'Come, come, madame,' the woman doctor said. 'All will be well! . . . You can be sure of that!'

Aunt Aline went back to her apartment. Françoise came and spoke to me in my room.

'Don't you worry, Fatoman,' she whispered. 'They're going to operate on you and then you'll soon be better . . . D'you hear me?'

'Yes. I hope so, too. But go away now, Françoise. Hospital visits are limited to a certain length of time. You must obey the rules.'

So that was how Françoise took her leave of me that day. The next morning, when she came to visit me, accompanied by her grandmother, I had already been operated on, and was lying in bed.

'Don't tire him,' said the nurse on duty. 'Your friend needs plenty of rest.'

'You should have telephoned me before operating on him,' Aunt Aline protested. 'I left my address with you.'

'I'm sorry about that, but we couldn't wait any longer. The doctor decided it was necessary to operate immediately.'

Stretched on a bed of pain, I spent two weeks of misery. Later, when I left the hospital, I had grown skinny, but I was cured, completely cured, of my illness.

After several months spent at my hotel in convalescence, I realized once and for all that Paris is not a French city but an international center in which human beings are grouped solely according to their intellectual affinities. I had not had this kind of feeling at all when I first arrived in Paris; what had struck me then was the surface appearance, the gray walls and skies—on the whole, the least important aspect of the place. I still knew nothing about the spirit of the city, nothing about the spirit of its inhabitants; nothing, or almost nothing, about Parisian *chic*, about French democracy—that liberty, that equality of all Frenchmen which, if it was not strictly true, nevertheless allowed everyone to express himself freely, to praise or to criticize anyone he liked. In the Colony, the white man is boss, the black man is his servant. Even though offices employ both whites and blacks, the boss and his employees mix very little, almost as little as the white boss and the black employee in Paris. The only difference is that in the Colony race constitutes the sole barrier, although the question of race is (apparently) not the matter at issue . . .

I had also come to notice that the concept of time, which until then had been unfamiliar to me, was here something precious and serious: time meant money. This country, unlike Africa, was a country in which charity began above all at home. A country, also, where those who did not have money had a hard time of it.

Once having entered this world of intellect and money, everything seemed to me not only different, but contrary. What had always seemed to me unimportant in Africa here held the center of the stage. What had until then seemed to me important was relegated to the background by the Parisian populace. What I considered evil in Africa was here considered good, and vice versa.

But I did not wish to lose myself forever in this different world, and while I lived there I was intent on preserving my identity. In that Paris where the cold, especially in winter, was so piercing, I would often put on my African boubou.

'But, Fatoman!' Françoise, offended, told me at her house one day, 'your attitude is not correct!'

'Why?' asked Aunt Aline, her grandmother.

'I do not think that rejecting everything he finds in Paris is the correct attitude for him,' she declared.

'Personally,' retorted Aunt Aline, 'I fail to see why a blind acceptance of occidental civilization should be a better attitude. If it were, he'd have to eliminate his entire past, which would mean sacrificing his identity. No one can reasonably be asked to make such a sacrifice.'

'I quite agree with you, grandmother,' replied Françoise. 'But all the same, Fatoman could dress as a European, especially in winter when it is so cold!'

But Aunt Aline replied, turning to me:

'I greatly admire the way you are dressed. I should like to see you in your native garb every time you come to see me.'

Pouting, Françoise protested:

'So you'd like to set up a little Africa here in the heart of Paris, grandmother!'

'Why not? The Chinese, the Vietnamese re-create their own countries here, by clinging to their native styles of dress and eating Chinese and Vietnamese food. Why shouldn't it be the same for Fatoman?'

'All right, all right!' I said, smiling, trying to calm them down. 'When I come to see grandmother I'll put on my boubou. And when I go out with Françoise I'll wear my European suit.'

They both burst out laughing. And each of them seemed to be satisfied by my proposal.

Time flowed by, peacefully, reassuringly. Thanks to Aunt Aline and Françoise, I was lucky to make the acquaintance of many people. Soon I no longer felt bored in Paris. I went out often. When my two friends and I took part in any of the French capital's festivities, people always admired my embroidered boubou and my velvet cap.

However, some gentlemen related to Aunt Aline came to call on me one day. I received them in the office of the hotel. A few minutes later these gentlemen and I had taken our seats in a black limousine which drove to the Rue de Varenne. They had told me:

'Young man, we should like your assistance.'

'Please excuse me,' I replied, hesitantly, 'this is an honor which I find difficult to accept. I have to attend school and complete my studies.'

'We have approached you,' they replied, 'to help us consolidate our fraternal Franco-African Union. Do you know our president?'

'Yes. Yes. I've attended his lectures more than once.'

'Then will you consent to participate in the realization of this great work?'

'Yes, for true Franco-African union, I am prepared to make every sacrifice.'

I spent the mornings at the Rue de Varenne. The afternoons I spent elsewhere, as a probationer. I was engaged in several activities. In the evenings I also took part in broadcasts. These diverse activities allowed me to make contact with cultivated men, and to further my education. Soon I was able to purchase a small car in which I drove all over Paris every free evening. During the holidays, I would drive down to the Côte d'Azur, to Spain; or go to Belgium, to Switzerland. It was an opportunity for me to get to know many countries and many people.

Then, one evening when I had gone to visit Aunt Aline and was talking about my eventual return to my native land, I came out with:

'The French are free. Completely free.'

'The reason why I devote my life to helping young Africans is really so that they may broaden their minds,' she answered. 'In particular, I want them to understand our social problems.'

'After the six years I have spent in Paris I realize better now that the colonized native is not a free man. Or at least not completely free. And now I can understand better the reasons why our people should rise up against colonial domination.'

'I love liberty, Fatoman,' she replied. 'Everyone loves to be free. But if one day the French *colons* in your country are to be replaced by men without moral standards, your country will be brought under a fascist regime, a dictatorship. Then, you will nostalgically recall the days of colonial domination, which will then appear to you in retrospect like a lost paradise. But it will be too late.'

'Too late?' I inquired.

'Yes, too late, because the *colons* will have come back to France.'

'Personally, I'm in a hurry to get back to Africa!' I declared. 'Any *colon* who tries to do me down had better look out! I know them now, these white men!'

Suddenly Aunt Aline looked indignant. And she began to make me a long speech:

'Fatoman,' she began, in an almost furious tone of voice, 'you claim you know now what white men are like. Doubtless you know something about us. Nevertheless, one never knows another person completely, and a race even less so. And none of us knows himself completely. Get this into your head: never forget that the ignoble things which have happened in your country have occurred quite independent of the will of the French people, and often of its governments. You know this perfectly well. Though the struggle has already started in Africa, the struggle which it has been agreed should be called the struggle of liberation, never forget that the enemy is not a race, is not the white man, but a gang of profiteers. Fight against that gang and entrust your country to reliable men, to men who have already shown their mettle: then you will open the gates of your country to the entire world, to all the intelligence and enterprise that may be found among all the people of the world, to all those qualities that urge people to conquer everything in the domains of the intellect, of art, of technology.'

'Yes, Aunt Aline, you are right, racism is idiotic. The racist is a man who has not achieved full intellectual and moral development. At bottom, he's an animal.'

'Then do you understand now that the men out there who are waging a systematic war against white men are in fact just animals?'

'I believe so. Your opinions are correct.'

Finally, one day, after innumerable negotiations, I obtained leave to visit Africa. These negotiations had been extremely difficult because it had been hoped I would remain in Paris, if not forever, then at least for a long time. But I would not be dissuaded. Some of them did not hesitate to come up to me and say: 'What's this? What's this we hear? You're going to leave us? Aren't you happy with us over here?'

I would invariably reply: 'I must go back.'

As I was preparing for my departure, I privately asked myself certain questions. Would life out there come up to my expectations? Although I was still young, I knew that things do not always happen exactly as one expects them to happen.

Often events go far beyond what one had ever dreamed or imagined, for reality is always complex.

All my Paris friends were there at the airport: Aunt Aline and Françoise never took their eyes from my face until the airplane took off. And there were tears, waved handkerchiefs. But above all, bumps over air

pockets and my usual airsickness. Finally, after a brief
stopover at Dakar, I reached Conakry.

Thus six years, six long years had sped by, divided
between the factory, the evening classes, midnight studies, and, from time to time, the company of Aunt Aline
and Françoise . . . And later, the Rue de Varenne and
the broadcasting studios.

After the six long years in Paris, fate arranged for a
visit, a brief visit, in Africa.

And so my first night in the village of my birth
was haunted by memories of Paris, memories that pur-
sued me everywhere, despite myself, and whose endless
stream prevented me from sleeping. . . .

Kouroussa

EARLY NEXT MORNING, I switched on my portable wireless set. Twiddling knobs in the dark, I managed to get Radio Conakry. Tino Rossi, Guétary and Mariano came on, singing one song after the other.

At the end of the program, they announced the times of arrival and departure of the banana boats. Just at that moment I should have liked to listen to a little classical music or to some African music: for example, to listen to the vibrant strings of the cora played by Kéba Sissoko, or the voice of Kouyaté Kandia. But this was just a dream, and as not as all dreams are transformed into reality, I had to content myself with what was offered.

'Turn the set down a bit,' said Marie, with a yawn, as she lazily stretched herself on the bed. 'It's not interesting. Wouldn't it be better to switch it off altogether?'

Lifting her head, she saw that I agreed with her, and, stretching out again, put out her hand and *click*! —snapped off the switch.

'It's always the same ones singing and talking,' she said. 'Instead of listening to the times of arrival and departure of boring banana boats, why don't we try to get a little more rest?'

She turned over and covered her head with her lino-cloth. I remained seated for a moment. Just as I was going to put out the storm lantern, a young man came into the hut. Raising my head, I saw my father beside him on the threshold.

'Good morning, my father!' I called to him.

'Good morning, Fatoman my son. This young man is one of the friends of your youth. He is called Bilali. Ever since yesterday he has been asking to see you.'

'Fine. That's fine,' I replied.

'Is there any rule,' I wondered, 'against receiving visitors so early in the morning?' But in my heart of hearts, I knew well enough that the youth had come out of pure friendship. At that moment I heard my mother's voice:

'Already up and about? . . . Aren't you feeling well, Fatoman my son?'

Afraid she might come in and see my nakedness, I hastily donned my caftan, seized a mat and sat down outside. Now we were seated with Bilali on my right and my father on my left. The latter, afraid that I might say something that would upset my mother, did not leave me time to answer. He answered for me:

'No, woman. He is not sick, he is simply tired. Our son's journey was a long one.'

'The journey was a long one,' I admitted, 'but I am not tired in the least.'

'And did you sleep badly?' my mother persisted.

'No. But all night long I was thinking of over there.'

'Oh!' she retorted. 'So you're already regretting having come to see us? Aren't you happy here?'

'Yes, I am. It was partly that happiness that prevented me from sleeping.'

My father remained seated, his legs neatly crossed, tailor fashion, like an Oriental. Further off, my mother remained standing. Was my father still afraid of hear-

ing me say something that might upset my mother?
Probably, because now he was watching over every
word I uttered and giving every phrase an appropriate
ring.

He ought to have known that I would take good care
not to say anything that could alarm my mother. She
had never approved of my departure for Europe. And
besides, she had always been very emotional. I knew
that. Bilali, on my right, hearkened to our conversation
without saying a word, but with a quizzical look on his
face.

'Is the country beautiful over there?' she inquired.

'Yes, superb. I'll show you some snaps.'

'Now, then, woman,' my father suddenly growled.
'Go and get the breakfast ready. The sun is already
high.'

My mother disappeared. When he was quite sure she
had gone away, my father approached me and whispered in my ear:

'Your comrades who came back last year told me
that life over there had been very hard for you. Is that
true?'

'Yes, it's quite true. But is not suffering the best
school? And besides, over there I met so many nice
people, and they helped me. Helped me very much.'

'Well, yes, my son, if one doesn't give up the ghost
in the process, one is hardened and strengthened and
tempered by suffering, like iron in the fire. May the
Lord be bountiful unto your friends over there!'

Again he leaned over and muttered in my ear, after
making sure that no one was listening, that no one was
slinking round the hut:

'Your mother must know nothing of all that. You
understand me?'

'I understand. She won't know a thing.'

'A man cannot tell a man's troubles to women,' he
said.

'Women,' commented Bilali approvingly, 'they're too sensitive.'

'That they are.'

Turning to my father, I asked him:

'What about you? . . . How have things been with you?'

'It's been a hard time,' he replied. 'But anyhow we were in our own house. While you! . . . You see, my trade is no longer worth very much. The shoemakers, and the jewelers like me, have all been practically condemned to unemployment. Now it's the Lebanese, coming in with their cheap-jack trash, and the shops are full of the junk. Because of the difference in price, our women prefer their muck to our golden jewelry, our leather bags tanned by our native cordwainers. So I have been devoting myself entirely to sculpture. The toubabs on their way through buy many of my statuettes. They're mad about them.'

I lifted my head. My friend Konaté, whom I had lost sight of since he had started studying to be a teacher, was coming into our concession. Now he was coming toward us:

'*Hérè Sira?* (Have you had a good night?)' he said.

'*Tana Massi!* (No ill fortune occurred during the night)' my father gave reply.

'*Dembaya Don?* (And how is your family?)' inquired Bilali.

'My family enjoys the very best of health,' replied Konaté.

'I am happy to see you,' I greeted him.

'And I likewise,' he replied, and went on: 'Yesterday, on my return from a political meeting, my woman told me of your arrival.'

'And is your wife enjoying the best of health?'

'She is enjoying the very best of health.'

'What about you?' I asked, turning to Bilali. 'What are you doing?'

'I am in the diamond trade. They're selling very well, now, diamonds! Not that the others are doing so well!' he declared. 'But as for myself, I cannot complain. All I have to do is to go to the mines, and I rake in millions. I've got the most extraordinary luck with precious stones.'

'So much the better for you,' said my father. 'I am always happy to see the comrades of my son making something for themselves in life.'

'I've bought a car,' Bilali added. 'You must see it! There's not another like it in Guinea.'

As I listened to him saying this last phrase, I felt I wanted to shut him up, for his boasting was getting on my nerves. I tried, with a gesture, to show him that vanity of that kind is unworthy of well-bred people. And as he did not understand my gesture, I hazarded:

'There was once a very rich man, but he had one very big enemy.'

'Who was that?' Bilali asked innocently.

'His own big mouth!' I retorted. 'The man I'm talking about was too boastful.'

He did not understand, or pretended not to, and went on as before hymning the praises of his car. My father, amused, had a mischievous smile on his face. Konaté, usually very talkative, had fallen silent. He was gazing openmouthed at Bilali.

'Oh, yes,' the latter was declaring, 'there isn't another car like mine in the whole of Guinea. Not even in the whole of Africa, the whole continent of Africa. It's the only one of its kind made in America. It was specially custom-made . . .'

'Specially custom-made for whom? . . . For you?' I said.

'No! Not for me. For the Liberian president. But as I was able to cough up twelve thousand dollars in cash—three times the normal price, I might say; there's nothing on this earth you can't get with money—the vehicle was handed over to me.'

This lie and that bragging, typical of the most vulgar *nouveau riche*, were really too crass and too childish. We burst out laughing. But Bilali continued unabashed:

'Each time I take my seat behind the steering wheel of my vehicle and drive into Kouroussa, the entire populace turns out to admire me. They almost prevent me from continuing, and only give way after I have given a demonstration of lowering and raising the roof of my United States of America automobile.'

'You're a real capitalist,' Konaté cried at last, shouting with laughter. 'A born capitalist, who has seen the light as if by divine accident in a land of proletarians. Don't you realize your place isn't here?'

'Where is my place?' Bilali demanded.

'In the United States of America,' Konaté laughed in reply.

'No,' my father said with an amused smile. 'He's not a capitalist. He's more of an *arriviste*. Capitalism has its qualities and its defects, but *arrivisme* has nothing but defects.'

'Instead of squandering so much money on a heap of ironmongery, you'd have done better if you'd first constructed a villa. A villa would have been more useful to a town like Kouroussa. A villa is a good investment.'

'I'll do that too, Konaté,' replied Bilali.

'It would perhaps have been better to start that way,' I commented. 'How can you stand going to bed in a hut with an earth floor when you know what it is to roll around in such a magnificent chariot? You should first of all have built yourself a solid dwelling place.'

But Bilali had an answer:

'I couldn't prove to my fellow citizens that I am rich by building a villa. A villa cannot be seen by everyone: it cannot be driven around the town. Whereas an automobile! . . .'

'Judging by your way of thinking, you're not a bit like the other comrades of my son,' pronounced my father.

But Bilali was irrepressible. We heard nothing but bragging and boasting. And already, after this very short time, we had become accustomed to his flow of words, to his way of turning his material wealth into a celebration—wealth acquired honestly or dishonestly (a diamond trafficker is hardly likely to be honest). Our laughter wakened Marie, who soon joined the swarm of my sisters and 'little sisters' in the kitchen. After a moment she re-appeared, this time carrying a big bowl of gruel. When she had set it before us, almost going down on her knees to show her respect for my father, her father-in-law, she retreated once more, on bare, silent feet, to the kitchen, where she rejoined my sisters and 'little mothers.'

We men, ladles in our hands, had already begun to sup the gruel.

'All of you here,' Bilali went on, swallowing a ladleful of hot gruel, 'have been to school. You have your diplomas, and one or several professions.'

'I never went to school, my boy,' remarked my father drily.

'I know, Da,' he answered. 'But you have several professions. As for me, I didn't get much further than the elementary school. Consequently my diplomas are my money and my convertible. If I don't display these acquisitions for all to see, people will take me for a no-good type.'

It amused us to hear him talking like that. Bilali thought he had saved his face. My father interrupted his flow and chivied him, saying:

'My boy, how long is it since you left these parts?'

'A long time. A very long time ago.'

'And what do you call a long time?' my father persisted.

'Fifteen years,' Bilali replied.

My father shook his head and chuckled mischievously. We had already stopped eating, but remained seated on the mat.

'Leave Bilali alone,' Konaté said, smiling. 'Time will one day teach him a lesson—at his own expense, unfortunately. And anyhow, we're not going to let him wait even that long. Fatoman and I will take him in hand and give him some lessons in morals. What about that, Bilali?' Konaté ended, defiantly.

Bilali, giving a loud laugh, replied:

'I'll gladly listen to your lecture on morals, but they won't change my way of thinking. Nor my convictions.'

We burst out laughing again. My father suddenly stood up, brushing down his boubou.

'Your company is most agreeable, my children,' he said. 'But I must take my leave of you. It's time to go to my workshop. Have a good day.'

'You have a good day, too,' we all answered.

'What about going for a walk?' Konaté proposed.

'All right. You wouldn't have any kola on you?'

'Yes, I have,' he said, offering me some.

After chewing it, I lit a cigarette. In the yard, one of my little sisters ran after me carrying a glass of water. I drank it. The water had that freshness and savor it always has after the bitter taste of the kola nut. We went strolling round the lanes of the village, and in the course of our promenade I asked Konaté:

'By the way, how's school going?'

'Oh, very badly,' he said.

'Why?'

'All this colonialism!'

I listened attentively. The phrase just uttered by Konaté was to be the forerunner of many more. I sensed this and so said nothing. I waited in silence until he should have revealed what was in his heart. Bilali also listened without saying anything.

'There's not much room in the school,' Konaté went on. 'It's not pleasant to see children who perhaps possess outstanding abilities running wild about the streets because there's no room, no places for them in the already overcrowded classrooms. I'm not denying the value of the efforts put out by our new educational directors. But one thing is certain: we need more schools.'

'It makes me feel sick,' I commented.

'It was this lack of places that caused me to leave school so soon,' said Bilali.

'At any rate,' said Konaté, 'the few pupils we do have work diligently. It's a consolation to see them getting down to their studies day after day. They often have to study far into the night even. But it is discouraging when the inspector from the Academy pays us a visit and tells us—ignoring the fact that our children have been swotting away all year without a break —that they know nothing at all compared with what pupils in France know, and that a child in arms over there knows far more than our children do.'

'Don't worry. He only said that in order to make them work harder.'

'I'm sure he did,' Konaté replied with an approving nod. 'But we teachers are troubled, deeply troubled, when we think of the future of our native land. We even wonder sometimes whether so much hard work will ever bring any benefits for the children here. The day will come when they will leave the elementary school, and the most talented of them will perhaps be admitted to modern technical colleges. But none of them will enter a university faculty, for the simple reason that there is no university in our country.'

I was still listening to him in a silence that was neither approving nor disapproving. But probably he did not notice this. There are people who do not know how to read the faces of others; they understand only the spoken word; my comrade Konaté belonged to this

category. As for Bilali—who had lost interest in the
discussion, since we were speaking French—he had
taken leave of us, promising to join us again at my
house when darkness had fallen. Konaté went on:

'Oh, I'm not saying all this for the pleasure of in-
veighing against the *colons*! There are, thank God,
many other pleasures, and that is one pleasure I do not
enjoy. I know too that Rome was not built in a day.
But the plain fact is that they call us French citizens
and refuse us education. Our country has very few
schools. The *colons* are not alive to the immense desire
to learn, the immense willingness in the hearts of our
scholars.'

'All that is a question of credit, therefore of budget.
And besides, you mustn't forget that we are passing
through the period of self-determination. Now it is we,
and not the *colons*, who are directing the affairs of our
land.'

'Only on the surface,' he countered doggedly. 'It
appears to be our people directing affairs. But in actual
fact it's still the *colons* in control.'

'What becomes of the pupils when they leave
school? That's an important question, perhaps the most
important of all those questions I keep coming up
against in Guinea, a land which, like all countries that
suffered under colonial domination, was swept by a
great gale of emancipation in the wake of the Second
World War. It's the Administration that is the great
temptation. That's not difficult to understand. Busi-
nesses do not pay, or in any case pay less than a job in
the Administration.'

And my friend sighed again as we continued our
stroll:

'Everybody wants to be a clerk! Doubtless it's fairly
natural that youthful ambition should manifest itself in
that way and that it should tend toward the pen-push-
ing occupations, despite the demands of industry for

technicians, and of commerce for skilled workers. It's very disheartening that technicians here are not taken seriously, that they are not paid a decent wage—all of which naturally sends them in the direction of administrative careers, after first having done good but unpaid work as qualified technicians.'

'I understand perfectly,' I said.

'Many, too, display a marked lack of enthusiasm for manual work.'

'No, Konaté,' I said. 'I cannot agree with that attitude.'

Konaté went on, spitting a shred of kola out:

'Yet this lack of enthusiasm is quite understandable. It is the result of low wages and lack of opportunity. And moreover, there's no future. At any rate, for those at the top of the ladder. Because at the bottom it's only a question of finding enough people . . .'

He went on: 'In fact, if wages were equal, a pupil leaving technical school would choose manual work. If we were in that technical school pupil's shoes, wouldn't we do the same? One should, in accepting a lower remuneration, at least have some hopes of better prospects in the future. But those better prospects cannot be hoped for, they are not there. And if the general training in administration these young people receive is better paid than work which makes use of their technical knowledge, it is inevitable that after a while they should choose the former.'

He lit a cigarette, pondered a while, then went on:

'It's sad to see the idea of filthy lucre mixed up with the question of education. Obviously, the purely material question, the question of money, is bound up with one's ideals to the extent that one can say: if money does not mean happiness, at least it contributes to it. But the school should, after all, have a more disinterested role to play. It should be based on a certain concept of the true nature of modern man, and be devoted entirely toward the development and the achievement of that ideal. But the masses understand it otherwise. That's the chief problem . . .'

We returned to the house after this rapid conspectus of the educational situation in our country.

That night was my second night in Kouroussa. It promised to be a memorable one. Konaté, who had taken his leave of me after we had returned from our walk, had later come back, accompanied by his wife. During the whole of my stay in Kouroussa he never left my side after that. Bilali too had come back. He had shut his shop at dusk and come to join our party. We did not get on too well together, but that did not matter to him. The important thing was that we had passed our childhood together. Because of that, he was to be in our company every evening. My little brothers and sisters as well as other young folk were there also. But I could not put names to all of them. I had left them when they were still very young, and now I did not always recognize them at once. But the witch doctor who, after the evening meal, had entered my hut knew everybody. In fact, ever since that morning, when he had been told of my arrival, he had been in a state of feverish excitement. He had brought his cora to play to us in my hut, and that was his own way, the best way of bidding me welcome home. He played a prelude on his instrument; then he began to chant the praises of every one of us: of Konaté first, then of Bilali and so on to each of the visitors, male and female, who that night thronged my hut. Each of us in turn heard the lofty deeds of his ancestors recalled in song. As the genealogical trees went on growing and spreading their branches, the witch doctor's *chéchia* or bowl, placed on the ground between his feet, filled up with coins which we tossed in every time he chanted something that flattered our vanity. The cora added to the beauty of his voice, accompanying his chronicles, decorating them with notes that were now mellow, now shrill. Marie, ensconced on the divan-bed in a corner of the hut, had listened eagerly to the couplets as they came rolling out: like the rest of us, she had relished the wonderful stories related by the witch doctor. But she was not satisfied with that. She wanted to hear her own tale, her very own story. Unable to wait any longer, she suddenly muttered to me:

'Fatoman, ask your witch doctor to tell the one about the jealous man.'

I had heard this story always with great enjoyment I don't know how many times.

As soon as the request had been made, Kessery the witch doctor stood up. His samba shirt* clung tightly to his well-upholstered figure. Clearing his throat, he began to tell the story. All eyes were fixed upon him.

'Moussa! Moussa! Moussa!' he suddenly shouted, as if inspired. 'Moussa, the jealous man, suffered deeply on account of his jealousy.'

Marie sat up, not wanting to lose one word of the recital. Looking at her, one could see that she was passionately involved in the tale, as she had been by none of the other stories previously related: for the subject was the jealousy of men and husbands.

The witch doctor, enthralled as much by the sound of his own voice as by the music of his cora, began his chanting.

'Once upon a time, there was a beautiful woman,' he began. 'She was very beautiful indeed, certainly the most beautiful woman in all the kingdom. She was called Habibatou and had for her husband a rich Imam by the name of Moussa, who possessed great herds of cattle and flocks of sheep, as well as rich and fertile

---

*A shirt with three pockets.

lands which stretched for many hundreds of leagues. And this Imam, Moussa, who led all the prayers in the Mosque, was a serious man indeed, therefore a man loved and respected by all the inhabitants of that kingdom.'

'It's a story about a rich and deeply religious man, and a woman as beautiful as a fay,' Marie broke in, as if prompting him.

The audience, deeply interested, listened with bated breath.

'Yes,' went on the witch doctor. 'But there was more to it than that. Above and beyond the woman's beauty and Imam Moussa's piety there was something else, something even more poignant. I am coming to it.'

'I am listening,' she answered, without taking her eyes from him.

'This man, the rich Imam, liked to keep an eye on his wife Habibatou, whom he forbade ever to leave the house. She had to send a woman servant even to make purchases in the market, for the jealous husband, Imam Moussa, would allow inside his house no servant of the masculine sex unless the latter had been castrated. This household, which had been living in peace for ten years, had three lovely sons, aged respectively nine, seven and five years.'

'So there were five people: the father, the mother and the three children?' Marie asked.

'Yes,' replied the witch doctor. 'But one day, that devout father, so close to his Lord, whom he called the King of Kings, asked his Lord and God in his prayers to show him some other woman as beautiful, as charming, as faithful as Habibatou.'

'Men! They're all the same!' cried Marie in surprise. 'He wanted a second wife! Didn't he have enough with the first, who was as beautiful as a fay and who was giving him sons?'

'No. To Imam Moussa, one woman, one wife only, was not enough. He wanted two.'

'And what did the King of Kings do?'

'Well, "Madam," the Lord, giving a great laugh, answered the Imam thus: "You may ask me, adorable human creature that you are, to give you a beautiful, charming and fertile woman, but do you ask me to give you one as faithful as your wife, for, adorable human creature that you are, *she* is nothing of the kind."'

The witch doctor paused for a moment, played a resounding solo on the cora, and then continued, to a muted accompaniment:

'Naturally Imam Moussa was indignant at this revelation, and to such an extent that his religious faith was almost shaken. But something very strong kept his religious beliefs intact. He cried: "My Lord, praise be unto thee, Creator of heaven and earth, of angels and devils, of water and fire, Creator of all things, King of all Kings, show me the light!" Then the Lord replied: "Very well. Tomorrow, before daybreak, I command thee to go into thy field. On the edge of the field, on the skirts of the forest, thou shalt climb the great tree that thou shalt see there, and thou shalt wait at the summit of that tree, concealed within its foliage. In the evening, thou shalt recount to me what thou hast seen."

'Imam Moussa, of course, carried out the instructions precisely. At the first crowing of the cock, there he was in the place the Lord had described, and hidden within the depths of the leaves. In the morning, as was the custom, dignitaries began to call at his house, some to pay courtesy visits, others to bring him gifts, and yet others for the sheer pleasure of seeing him.

' "My husband is out," Habibatou would say to each one of them, though she herself did not know where he had gone. "Perhaps he has gone to pray at the Mosque," she would add, to reassure the visitors. The faithful would depart, and return somewhat later, only to find Imam Moussa still absent.

'Soon the muezzin was summoning the faithful to the Mosque for the first prayers of the afternoon.

Imam Moussa was still away from home. They began
to feel worried about what might have happened to
him, but as nothing was allowed to interrupt prayers,
his subordinate took his place and presided over the
worship. And people said: "He's a wise man. Imam
Moussa is a wise man. Doubtless he has gone to se-
quester himself in some quiet place to read passages
from the Koran. Let us wait a while longer; if he does
not come back by this evening we shall begin to look
for him."

'As for his wife, Habibatou, she had prepared suc-
culent dishes. As soon as the streets were deserted,
when everyone was at the Mosque, she made sure that
no one was watching her and then, on noiseless feet,
left the house and ran to the field. Five o'clock had just
sounded, and the sun, his strength already gone, was
not far from setting.

'Habibatou sat down in her accustomed place of
assignation. It so happened that this was at the foot of
the great tree in which her husband was hiding. A few
moments later, after she had called three times and the
forest had sent back three times the echo of this pre-
arranged signal, a man appeared in the distance. When
he had drawn nearer, she recognized the shepherd who
guarded the herd of cattle and the flock of sheep belonging to Imam Moussa. It was her lover: a man in
rags, hideous, a dwarf, poorly built. Anyone seeing him
might have thought he wasn't a human being but a
gorilla.

'Soon, on reaching the foot of the great tree, what
should he do, the shepherd, that hideous specimen of
humanity, but begin to shout thus: "I'll thrash you!
You're making a fool of me! What were you doing? . . .
I've been waiting for my dinner since noon! I'll whip
you!" . . .

'The shepherd stooped down to tear from a bush a
springy branch to use as a whip, while the woman,

distressed, knelt down before him and bowed her head to the ground, crying: "Yes, beat me! You are right! It is I who am wrong." And she lifted her skirts and bared her back for the lash of the whip.

' "Who's the master?" the herdsman went on. "Is it the Imam or me?"

' "You are the master, not he!" the woman replied.

' "Dang it all, I don't believe you! I'm beginning to believe that he's your master, and not me!" the shepherd went on.

' "Master, I beg of you, have pity on me!" the woman moaned. "The Imam has been out since early morning; I have been waiting for him but have not seen him come back. And just when everyone had gone to the Mosque, I ran out to bring you your meal."

' "You're lying!" shouted the shepherd.

' "I swear to you!" she cried. "He's away from home. I did not want to leave the house with no one there. So many dignitaries and visitors come to see him! . . ."

' "All right, then!" the herdsman growled. "Get up."

'Trembling with terror, the woman rose to her feet. She loved her shepherd so much that she did not want to do anything to upset him.

' "I beseech your forgiveness," she added, in a fresh access of fear.

' "All right, all right, I believe you. We've been together now ten years. I know you have never lied to me."

'And the two lovers were reconciled.'

Once again the witch doctor stopped chanting. He played a long solo on his cora before continuing his tale.

'During this time,' he went on, 'Imam Moussa, perched up in his tree, had been a horrified witness of this scene. At the top of the tree, he had parted the leaves and gazed down upon his wife: she was the most beautiful of all the women in the region, and the richest also. She enjoyed a style of life beyond compare. And she was the wife of the Imam, a woman admired and respected by everyone. Then he had looked at the shepherd, that dwarf whom he had taken on more out of pity than of necessity. Finally he thought of himself, of the part he played in society; of the respect that was accorded him; and he said to himself: "That man who is making love to Habibatou is not worth my little finger. He's a nobody. I don't understand."

'And perched at the top of the tree, in a low voice, in a very low voice, he rendered thanks unto his Lord: "*Allahou akbar!*"*

'But down below, at the foot of the tree, the fun and games were still going on. The shepherd had seated himself beside Habibatou and laid his left arm tenderly about her shoulders whilst with the right he began to shovel the rice into his mouth. At the end of a quarter of an hour he had wolfed the lot.

' "Go home now . . . Your food was delicious, more delicious than all the meals you have offered me during the past ten years. But hurry back home. Your zebra (the Imam) might be getting worried about you."

' "Go where?" Habibatou moaned.

' "Home, of course. Back to your zebra!"

'But Habibatou, panting for love, had been expecting something more.

' "I understand!" she cried. "You're getting rid of me. You're holding it against me . . . You're angry because I came late just now."

' "Not so, my girl. But your husband might come back before you. Then you would run the risk of being scolded."

' "You're lying!" she screamed. "You're trying to get rid of me! Well, now it's up to you to prove to me that you don't hold anything against me."

'After she had finished speaking, she removed her
*Allah alone is great.

loincloth and spread it on the ground; her bodice too. Now she was standing upright in all the splendor of her nakedness. And seen thus, she appeared even more beautiful than before. Her smile was much more bewitching than when she had been wearing clothes. One might even have said that those garments—scarf, loincloth and bodice—had made her ugly. She was beautiful in the African sense of the word, bearing upon her body the twelve signs of beauty: white teeth, slender neck (a long neck garlanded with little folds of flesh), narrow heels, fine hands, sloping shoulders, broad pelvis, long, thin forearms . . .

"The husband, perched at the top of his tree, nearly fell down. He had to hold on tightly to prevent himself from falling, so beautiful did his wife Habibatou appear to him then—Habibatou, whom he approached only at night, when their three sons were abed and asleep, and who now seemed to him suddenly more beautiful and more exciting than ever. It was the first time he had caught her in an immodest attitude, abandoning herself in a manner that was not displeasing to him, but which on the contrary attracted him. But this was not his moment: the place of honor was reserved for the shepherd at the foot of the tree—*he* was the chief actor now! The lover waited some time, for he wanted to be sure that no one was prowling about nearby, that no one would see him. "There's no one about," he said to himself, and advanced upon her. His heart was beating wildly, very wildly, the more so because the shape he saw lying before him on the ground was very seductive; and besides, what he was about to perform was not altogether permissible. Certainly he was not altogether inexcusable, and he might even be said to have reason enough and to spare for servicing this fay who had come of her own free will to importune him in the wilds. "If I were to be caught," he suddenly thought, "I should cut a pretty poor figure all the same. The law would not be on *my* side." But neither was it a risk he could refuse to take. "If one doesn't run risks like that," he thought to himself, "there's no pleasure left in life." And he took the risk. He knelt down, and bared his utter nakedness in the same immodest manner as his girl . . .

'Imam Moussa, perched at the top of his tree, discreetly parted the leaves in whose depths he was concealed. What he now witnessed at the foot of the tree was unbearable. Distraught with anger as well as with anguish, he furtively turned his head aside and sank his teeth into the branch on which he was crouching. He squeezed his eyes tight shut. But from the foot of the tree a sound of panting sobs and sighs reached him. These sounds grew weaker and weaker as time went by. Finally they stopped altogether; as if everything down below had grown calm; as if the flames that had been kindled had now been extinguished . . .

'Later, the Imam once more parted the leaves and cast a glance at the shepherd and Habibatou. Everything was again in order: Habibatou had donned her garments as if nothing had happened, and the hideous shepherd had put on his verminous rags.

'Imam Moussa understood then that the King of Kings is never wrong, never wrong. At the top of his tree, he paid homage to the fullness of the divine power.'

'Well, then,' Marie interrupted him, 'you mean to say that all women are like your fay?'

'No,' the witch doctor boldly answered. 'I simply want to prove that keeping a strict eye on a woman is a waste of time. In my opinion, if a woman wants something, God wants it for her. Even shut up in the house, a woman will always do as she pleases.'

'There you are, now,' she said, turning toward me. 'Are you going to keep a strict eye on me all the time?'

'Oh, no! I shan't keep an eye on you at all. Like the

witch doctor, I find that kind of surveillance ridiculous, and besides, I trust you.'

'But what solution would you suggest, witch doctor,' she said, 'for a problem such as you have just described?'

'A solution? I can't see any. I believe one must know how to arouse and keep one's woman's love—flatter her, and direct the affairs of the household in a spirit of mutual confidence. When the wife loves her man, she become an angel and remains faithful. When she does not love him, she is transformed into a demon capable of anything. Therefore we see that in every woman on earth there is both an angel and a demon.'

'Hearty thanks—from the women of the world!' she retorted sourly.

Then, raising her voice again, she inquired:

'But then what happened to your Imam?'

'Well, when evening came, he slunk back to his house and said nothing to anyone. Even his wife was unable to read any change in his expression. He acted as if nothing had happened. He even joked with his wife, who was also as charming as usual. Only when it was completely dark and he had said his prayers did the Imam ask his Lord to show him a little more light . . . He waited some time. Finally a voice of great majesty broke the silence of his meditations:

' "Has thou not three sons, adorable human creature?"

' "Yes, my Lord," replied Imam Moussa, gazing about him as if trying to catch sight of the person whose voice he heard, as if hoping to see God himself. But what could he expect to see or discover in his surroundings? . . . Is God visible? . . . No! He is not! . . .

So, gazing ahead of him, with his eyes fixed on emptiness and nothingness, he again heard the same voice of great majesty, saying unto him:

' "Only one of them is from thy loins. The two others are sons of the shepherd."

' "Ah, my Lord!" he exclaimed, "I believe in thee and in thy omnipotence, but I am convinced that all three sons are issued from my loins! They are my own flesh and blood, they are as alike as three drops of water, and all resemble me! Oh, all-powerful God, mightest thou not be mistaken?"

'Imam Moussa, in saying his prayers, had abandoned himself entirely to his Lord. In order to prove his utter humility before the divine power, he had tied a rope round his neck, and was like an animal, yes, a quadruped, with a halter. He had tied the other end of this rope to a hook in the wall. And he told the King of Kings everything; he had confessed to him all the errors he had committed here below on this wretched earth, and everything his human conscience reproached him with. Now he was, if not more pure, at least as pure as a child. His individual soul was pure, pure with the purity of the universal soul, with the purity of God's own image . . . This was the ideal state in which to receive the grace of the King of Kings, he thought.

'Seated on a prayer mat, his legs crossed tailor-fashion, like an Oriental, his eyes fixed upon the ceiling, he remained there with both hands extended, as if waiting for something to drop upon him from above, as if waiting for the grace of heaven to descend upon his brow.

'He waited a fairly long time in that position, believing that something would certainly happen. But nothing happened.

' "The Lord," he thought, "no longer has eyes for me! Oh thou whom I love and whom I have adored all my life, canst thou no longer even hear my voice?" he asked in a low murmur, as if his faith in God had been shaken. Disappointed, profoundly and unpleasantly disappointed, his eyes awash with tears, he turned away his gaze from the ceiling and mechanically lowered his head, as if never expecting to hear anything again from the King of Kings, as if hoping for nothing, nothing more from his Lord.

' "The King of Kings does not even hear my voice!" he murmured, and began to pray again. "If he does not hear my voice, perhaps it is because I did not call him by his true name. God is just like a real human being, and so he too has his own personal name, given him at birth. He baptized himself and gave himself that particular name; as long as one does not utter that name, he refuses to reply." So he continued to pray, this time uttering what he believed to be the real baptismal name of the King of Kings.

'Just when he was least expecting it, a terrifying noise, a fantastic sound, suddenly interrupted his contemplations. It was as if the house that sheltered him had collapsed and tumbled to the ground. Surprised and frightened, he raised his head and realized that the ceiling was no longer there, that the roof of his house was no longer there either. It was as if a mysterious force, a divine power, had snatched them away. And now the Imam's gaze soared directly to the stairway of heaven, was lost in the immensity of the starry vault . . .

' "Glory to thee, my Lord!" he prayed, mastering his fear. "I am convinced that thou art the sole Master of the Universe and that the Prophet Mohammed is thy chosen emissary!" Then he added: "I am convinced that the power thou dost wield, on high heaven and everywhere, is very great, is infinitely greater than the sign which thou has just revealed unto me. I know that this sign is as nothing, nothing but a symbol of the power thou dost wield and that is even more astounding, infinitely more astounding, than the vanishing of my ceiling and of the roof of my dwelling place."

'But as he was bringing to an end his praises to the Lord, the homage he was rendering to the omnipotence of the King of Kings, he once more lowered his head and beheld, to his great astonishment, a creature crouching before him; a kind of creature he had never, never seen in his life before.

'It could have been an angel, and indeed it really was

an angel, for this creature was extraordinarily beautiful; moreover, it was winged, and its great pinions of silver and diamonds sparkled like hosts of suns. This creature was so beautiful and so impressively brilliant that the human eye could not behold its magnificence for more than thirty seconds without blinking.

'The angel was wearing a white pipao* which completely covered its lower extremities, so that it was quite impossible to imagine what on earth they looked like.

' "Was it thou who didst call upon the King of Kings?" the angel demanded.

' "I don't understand!" babbled Moussa.

'For the angel had couched its question in literary Arabic, which the Imam did not understand, because he could not catch the meaning of all the words.

' "Ah!" cried the angel. "Dost thou not speak Arabic? What tongue dost thou speak? I speak all languages."

' "I speak the Konianké* tongue."

' "What can I do for thee?" the angel asked, speaking in the konianké tongue. "I am the envoy plenipotentiary extraordinary of the King of Kings, come hither to hearken unto thee and to give thee satisfaction."

'Imam Moussa, seated on his prayer mat could see the angel distinctly; or rather, he would dart glances at him from time to time, for there emanated from this angel, as I have already said, such sunbursts of effulgence that no mere mortal being could gaze upon him continually. And the Imam again bethought himself that the Lord is indeed astounding in the manifold diversity of his creations.

' "Well, it's like this," he replied. "I can't understand how two of my three children can be natural sons."

*Garment worn by the Mohammedans of Black Africa.
*People of the forest regions of Guinea.

' "On the morrow," declared the angel in a ringing, metallic, authoritative voice, "on the morrow, at the hour of the partaking of food, I conjure thee to strike fear into the breasts of thine offspring, yea, verily, admonishing them that the good Lord hath commanded thee to slaughter them. And behold, they that are not issued from thy loins shall flee away and, by this sign thou shalt know they are not thine." '

'But look here,' Marie broke in, 'why not have had them examined by a doctor? In that sort of case, a blood test would have settled everything!'

'Yes,' the witch doctor gave answer, 'you are doubtless right. But I am speaking to you now about an era when such medical practices were still unknown.'

'I want to hear the end of the story. Go on!' she commanded in an eager voice.

The witch doctor went on with the story, accompanying it with muted notes of the cora:

'Scarcely had he finished speaking, than the angel vanished; first a quarter of him disappeared, then half, then three quarters, then everything.

'With him vanished also the extraordinary radiance or "radiation" . . . But what about the ceiling? When he lifted his head, the Imam saw that the ceiling had come back into place. The roof too . . .

'The next day, when the sun stood at its zenith, shooting down its hot spears of light, and when the children gathered round the rice bowl, Imam Moussa burst into the room and, unsheathing his saber, threw it into the air and caught it again, shouting: "Make haste! . . . The good Lord stands in need of your souls. And I desire to see your blood flow. I must sacrifice you this instant!"

'The two elder sons, seeing their father suddenly become an executioner, took fright; one dropped his spoon in the dish; the second, panic-stricken, not only let fall his spoonful of rice which he was just raising to his lips, but spat out the food he already had in his gullet.

'The two older boys wanted to scream and run away, but the realization that their father would catch them at once glued them to the spot.

'Strangely enough, the youngest son, taking no notice of what was going on, continued to eat, and with such relish that it appeared he did not comprehend the threats uttered by his father. All the same, he understood them well enough. He could see the blade of the saber glittering, and its keenly whetted cutting edge: he realized his father was in no normal state of mind.

'When the meal was over, Imam Moussa raised the saber high above his head, and made as if to decapitate the three children. They fled in horror, with a great clatter of feet. But the youngest ran only a few steps, stopped, turned round and came back to his father, saying: "Kill me. Kill me. I'm not afraid."

' "It's all right, all right, thou true son of mine," said the Imam. "Thou art safe, and I shall not touch a hair of thy head."

'He took him up in his arms and gave him further assurances. As for the two older ones, they were still running. They could no longer trust their father, and could not believe it was a joke. They ran as fast as their legs could carry them.

' "And yet, those boys running away are as like me as two drops of water!" Imam Moussa told himself, in his secret heart. "Resemblance is not sufficient proof. Their mother, during her pregnancies, lived with me most of the time. That explains how the resemblance came about."

'He went back to the house, went to see Habibatou, still as beautiful, still as bewitching as ever, and suddenly decided to repudiate her.

' "From now on," he said, "you are no longer my wife. Collect your things and return to your parents."

'The dignitaries arrived, and the usual visitors. Displaying all their kindness and good sense, they listened to the wife's complaints. But the deceived husband refused to give ear to them; he took refuge in absolute silence, so that the dignitaries and distinguished visitors could not prevent the inevitable shipwreck of the marriage, and a divorce was granted.

'The woman packed her things and went back to her parents' house.'

While the witch doctor had been talking, Marie had watched him with a look of utter absorption, as if a moving film of the story she was listening to had been run before her mind's eye.

'But after that,' she said, 'what happened? What happened after the divorce?'

'Of course, each of them remarried. Imam Moussa's new spouse gave him a pretty little girl, named Kadidia. I do not know anything about the later life of his ex-wife Habibatou. Did she start meeting her shepherd again? Probably.'

'But was Kadidia, born of that second marriage, truly the child of Imam Moussa?' Marie wanted to know.

'Yes, it was his true daughter, issued from his loins. And strangely enough, in order to prevent her from acquiring female defects of character, he decided to feed her on cow's milk, and then to supervise her education personally. Kadidia was never allowed to sleep with her mother, but always in her father's hut, until she reached puberty.'

'What a queer way to go on!' Marie complained.

'Yes, it's very queer,' the witch doctor agreed with her.

'But why did he do such a thing?' the audience wanted to know.

'Ostensibly to shield Kadidia from the vices of the female sex.

'But is it sufficient,' he went on, 'to educate a girl in

a masculine environment in order to rid her of all
feminine instincts, to wipe out her deepest instincts?
Imam Moussa was soon to be given the answer to this
question. For one day, in fact, when Kadidia had
reached puberty and had become a really delicious little bud of a young woman, worthy of being loved, she
accompanied her respected father to the capital of their
kingdom, for the king had called upon him to render
some service or other . . .

'And what happened? I'm sure that's the question
you're all wanting to ask me now. Well, this rich and
powerful king, who governed his kingdom with an authority that could never be gainsaid, and an immense
and prosperous kingdom at that, had but an only son,
who by great misfortune, had been born a dwarf and
an idiot, incapable of imposing his authority upon the
royal court itself, not to speak of even the smallest
village in the kingdom. The king, in despair, had called
upon Imam Moussa, telling himself that the latter,
such a great believer and a master of the Koran, might
be able to persuade the Lord to give the Prince a normal body and a mind capable of issuing commands.

'While Imam Moussa was staying at the court,
where he occupied his own suite of chambers, the
queen fell madly in love with him. She loved the man
to distraction, so much so that she could not stop
herself from telling him of her passion, and repeating it
every time she found herself alone with him. But each
time Moussa respectfully informed her that he had not
come to pay court to the queen, but only to carry out
the mission that had been assigned to him. But the
greater the resistance the Imam offered the queen, the
more charming and seductive she made herself, so that
in the end it became difficult, if not downright impossible, to fend off such persistent temptation.

'As for his treatment for the prince, heir to the
throne, Imam Moussa requested the king to assemble
all the inhabitants of his kingdom on the esplanade

situated at the entrance to the royal palace; this was done immediately.

'When the entire population had been assembled on the vast esplanade, Imam Moussa asked that the prince should be requested to mount the platform placed in the center, so that all the people might see and follow the progress of the ceremonial which was to take place.

'Just when everyone had his eyes fixed on the platform and when an embarrassed silence began to hover round him, Imam Moussa, continuing to recite his prayers, enfolded the prince, using majestic gestures, in a mat of plaited osiers, a proceeding which hid him entirely from the sight of the spectators. No one said a word; the silence became all the more weighty and disquieting, and more and more strained, because the people had no idea what was going to happen.

'And then suddenly, like lightning, Imam Moussa whipped away the mat. And the people were stupefied to see, instead of the idiot dwarf, a handsome young man with an enigmatic smile, a fine young man as tall as the king himself.

' "Behold your prince!" Imam Moussa cried. He was unable to finish the phrase, for the people, howling with joy, had drowned it with their massed shouts of happiness. The king himself could hardly believe his eyes. Overwhelmed with emotion, he began to weep. And he breathed a sigh of relief that, even should he be taken from the throne by death, nothing now could prevent the kingdom from continuing to enjoy royal sway.

'The people dispersed, everyone going back to his village in a great babel of voices, discussing the spectacle and commenting with ecstasy on the prince's extraordinary beauty.'

'But then,' Marie intervened, 'the king must have given the Imam an enormous reward?'

'Yes! That evening, at the hour between the last

meal and bedtime, he had the Imam called into his presence. This was to inform him that on the morrow, when the sun had risen and its beams were beginning to warm the morning air, Moussa would receive from the sovereign, in the presence of all the notables and counselors of the crown, a well-deserved gift: a chest crammed with gold and diamonds.

'But at the bedtime hour, when Imam Moussa and his daughter Kadidia had reached their apartments and everyone had gone to sleep, the queen, under cover of darkness, slipped into their chamber.

' "I am come, Excellency," she began, "to pay you my adieus and to thank you for having made such a remarkable man of my son the prince. I am now very proud of him. His majesty the king intends—but doubtless you already know this—to recompense you on the morrow. Your departure will take place a few hours later. I, too, have prepared in your honor a small gift, which I should like to offer to you now. Pray follow me."

'But was it really in order to give him a present? Probably she really was going to give him a gift, one very different from what he would receive from the king. Was she not willing to offer him her naked body?

Imam Moussa, wearing nothing but a simple loin-cloth, followed her automatically (without even suspecting what was going to happen to him); the queen, like a real fay of legend, knew just how to handle matters. She, too, slipped off her loincloth and her bodice and then stood before him in a fascinating state of total nakedness, a nakedness which no man alive could have possibly resisted . . . And His Excellency Imam Moussa succumbed to the tantalizing provocation. He spent the night with the queen; a night so sweetly exhausting that . . . he overslept!'

'Overslept in the queen's bedchamber? . . . Next

morning he must have got a thorough trouncing instead of the chest filled with gold and diamonds!' Marie hopefully exclaimed.

'No, he did not. And you'll see why.

'That morning, when all the counselors and grand notables were congregated together about the presence of the king, and when they started calling for the Imam, for Imam Moussa, to present him with the promised gift, the Imam was still soundly sleeping in the arms of the queen! . . . And that delicious bud of all budding womanhood, his daughter Kadidia, brought up free of all feminine influence, was sitting uneasily in the bedchamber where she usually slept by her father's side. Perhaps her feminine instinct had already aroused in her a suspicion about where her father might be found at that moment, for she sat there with lowered head, as if in disgrace, right at the back of the bedchamber, where only scanty rays of morning sunshine succeeded in penetrating.

'Once again the call went forth for the Imam, for Imam Moussa, but there came no reply. Then, when the most venerable of all the notables had been charged with the task of going and deferentially waking him, Kadidia, that delicious bud of all budding womanhood, who had preserved in all their purity her feminine instincts, even though brought up free of all feminine influence, Kadidia, the flower of all maidenhood, found a solution in a flash.

' "I am as tall as my Da!" she said to herself in a low voice, as if trying to screw her courage up. "I shall disguise myself as a man and show myself thus to all the court, and they will take me for my Da."

'She put her idea into execution without delay. Wearing her father's pipao and shod in his babouches, assuming the paternal prayer cap and taking up his whip of office, she looked every inch a man. Though it would be better to say: she looked the spitting image of

Imam Moussa. With stealthy steps she left the bed-chamber, and, her head lowered, rapidly passed through the throng of royal notables and counselors without replying to any of their salutations, for it goes without saying that she did not want anyone to hear the tones of her woman's voice. Moreover, as she could imitate the deportment and the majestic bearing of Imam Moussa, no one in that gathering of royal nota-bles and counselors could ever have suspected that it was a woman passing among them, that it was the daughter of the Imam, the delicious bud of all budding womanhood, disguised as her honorable father.

'Indeed, several notables of the court, on the con-trary, approved of this behavior, saying: "This Imam is a person of the utmost correctness. Before coming to pay us his regards, he first wishes to present his re-spectful early morning homage to the queen."

'Having thus traversed the courtyard, the girl in dis-guise, Kadidia, entered the queen's apartments. She vigorously shook her father awake, for he was still in the arms of Morpheus, and got him on his feet. Then, with a conspiratorial whisper, she said in his ear:

' "Here are your clothes. Everyone's waiting for you outside. Before long they will realize that you have been sleeping with the queen. Hurry, for heaven's sake, hurry, put on your clothes and your shoes! . . . Don't forget the prayer cap! . . . Here it is! . . . Flay me with this whip of office. And don't stop to ask why; I'll explain everything later."

'Imam Moussa obeyed without a word; he swiftly adjusted his loincloth and pipao, put on his white prayer cap, stepped into his shoes and then gave Ka-didia a taste of the whip of office—Kadidia, who was waiting only for that in order to play the best scene in this comedy of which she was the author:

' "Honorable notables, comfort my Da! Comfort my Da!" she screamed, pretending to weep. "He always forbade me to spend the night with anyone else but himself . . . Even with a woman!" she went on, screaming even more loudly. "I spent last night sleeping with the queen!" she shrieked, piling scandal upon scandal as best she could.

'The notables, naturally, unable to make anything, anything at all, of this scene, this fine piece of farce, rushed to Imam Moussa, who was walking toward them, simulating anger. They comforted him with pleasant words, which he hearkened unto willingly, without saying one word, but all the same without granting the pardon all at once, in order to give the queen time to appear dressed and in her right mind. Like all women dressing, she took a long time about it, but finally appeared on the scene. She helped the notables to comfort Imam Moussa.

' "For the love of merciful heaven," she beseeched him, "pardon your daughter. We both sat up late last night. She wished to go and sleep in your bedchamber, but I dissuaded her. And finally, she dropped off. Forgive me, Excellency."

'Imam Moussa, apparently desolate, but smiling in his heart of hearts at the fortunate outcome of his awkward adventure, granted the pardon asked of him.'

'It's an extraordinary tale,' commented Marie.

'Extraordinary,' echoed Bilali.

'And did the notables and counselors never catch on to the trick?' Konaté asked.

'No,' replied the witch doctor. 'They never found out. They never knew that the Imam had spent the night with the queen. This story only goes to show that it's useless to keep watch and ward over a woman.'

'It also proves,' Marie hastened to say, trying to get the last word, 'that in every man there hides both an angel and a demon. For Imam Moussa, with his reputation for seriousness and piety, was unable to resist the queen's advances.'

'Many thanks—from the men of the world!' I threw at her with a laugh.

Bilali was radiant with happiness. When the story of Moussa came to an end, he pulled out of his pocket a thousand-franc note, which he handed to Kessery the witch doctor.

'Here you are, witch doctor,' he told him, 'I was happy this evening, really happy, to have heard the story of my ancestors. I had already heard it recounted by other witch doctors, but never with so many fine nuances, with so much eloquence. Thank you also for the tale about Moussa.'

'Thank you, thank you again, N'diati Bilali,' the witch doctor replied. 'But present a boubou to your witch doctor. Your ancestor gave horses to all my ancestors. I am no horseman. But a boubou! A pretty embroidered boubou, to hide the shame of my nakedness, is all I want.'

We burst out laughing. That is the way witch doctors go on, after all. They are never satisfied. They are never contented with the gifts we make them. They always have to ask for more, always more than they are given.

'Tomorrow, come to my shop. I shall present you with a great embroidered boubou, a fine boubou embroidered in the style of Foutah.'

'Ohôn! Ohôn! N'diati Bilali! Kanté, Kanté, your ancestor Soumaoro would have done no less! Kanté, Kanté!' cried the witch doctor. 'Tomorrow I shall call upon you at dawn to receive from your own noble hands my fine embroidered boubou.'

On that note the evening drew to a close. I accompanied my friends back to their homes.

On my way back to my hut, the field of cotton had flowered; no one had reaped it.*

---

*Malinké expression which means: 'The night was asparkle with stars. The night was a field full of stars.'

In the Workshop

THE DAYS SPED BY. And already I was thinking about my return to Paris. I wanted to purchase some objects made by native workmen in the town: a crocodile leather bag, some belts of tanned leather, to take to Aunt Aline.

One morning I decided to go shopping with Konaté. It was September; and schoolteachers are still on holiday there in the month of September.

So, we went down into the town. The streets were very lively, and the iridescent tunics of the women were in harmony with the serene sky. All the women we encountered were wearing these gay materials, multicolored, but now, to my eyes, too garish. I had been living for six years in Europe; for six years I had not been back to my native land; I was no longer accustomed to this orgy of colors.

We interrupted our stroll to enter a shoemaker's, then a second, and a third . . . There were no crocodile leather handbags, no belts or cigarette cases of tanned leather. These shops did not even have on sale a few of our cheap local wares. The shoemakers were squatting with folded arms, or cobbling up pairs of old shoes.

We left their shops in a rage. In a fourth shoemaker's we lingered a while, feeling almost certain that they must have some leather goods hidden away and that I might be able to buy some of them.

'Do you have such a thing as a handbag in tanned leather?' I asked the cordwainer innocently.

Konaté followed me into the shop, saying nothing. But the cordwainer just stared at me in stupefaction; his mouth set in a bitter line.

'What kind of thing is that?' he said, feigning not to understand me.

'I should like to buy one or two handbags of crocodile, some belts, some snakeskin cigarette-cases, hand-made by yourself.'

Again the cordwainer stared at me with a blank expression; then, without saying a word, he lowered his head. He kept his eyes lowered on the big cobbler's needle with which he was patching up some old shoes. Some customers entered from time to time—Europeans for the most part—gazed at the empty shelves and then left without saying anything.

I watched the cordwainer's mouth taking on an even more bitter expression; my continued presence disturbed him. Suddenly he raised his head and gave me a questioning look that was also full of hatred. His bitter mouth seemed to say: 'No, there's nothing. Ever since the Lebanese came bringing their trash, naturally ten times cheaper than our crocodile bags, our customers have fallen off. And there's nothing else left for us to do than to cobble up old shoes.'

After a while, as if he had seen quite enough of us standing there in his workshop, he got up, went through the door at the back and disappeared into his concession.

Somewhat disappointed, I left, followed by Konaté, and questioned one of the apprentices sitting on the veranda:

'Where can I buy some handbags of crocodile leather?'

'Our lives have been made a misery by these Lebanese who bring in a lot of flashy junk, which is preferred by our women because of the cheaper prices. Now they want us to sell them croco stuff at the same price as the Lebanese rubbish. They forget we have to go hunting, shoot the crocs, tan their hides and finally work it by hand. It works out dear that way. Do you belong to Kouroussa?'

'Yes. Only I haven't been back here for a long time.'

'Ah, that's why you're so hard to please. Heard you talking to my master . . . No, monsieur, there's nothing here at the moment. We are no longer making croco bags, or snakeskin belts and cigarette cases. We have nothing, nothing! But those dirty Lebanese, our enemies, can go on ruining our business as long as they like (they have plenty of money and sales outlets); they can go on boycotting our native crafts, but we won't give in. Those people are like cyclones that root up giant trees. But we craftsmen aren't trees . . . we are like lianas. What can the strength of a cyclone do against lianas? It can only play with them, shake them, twist them. Despite its extraordinary force, no cyclone can tear up or break lianas.'

'Perhaps we'll find some crocodile handicrafts and snakeskin goods further on. Or more likely, we won't find a thing in the whole of Kouroussa.'

And this was the opinion expressed by the apprentice cordwainer as we took our leave of him.

After we had walked around for quite a long time, and had passed the crossroads and climbed Samakoro Hill, we suddenly found ourselves in the market, or at any rate among a collection of stalls. This was the market, of course, but a market from which all native craft objects and local merchandise had disappeared; a

disappearance we had been afraid of ever since taking
our leave of the apprentice cordwainer. There was
nothing but cheap junk in the market, a lot of frippery
and trash imported from Europe and the New World.
A few earthenware pots made by women of the plains
and transported with difficulty to Kouroussa, a few
pearl objects made locally were the only proofs that my
town had still not entirely renounced its ancestral
arts.

Depressed, we turned to go home. There were no
taxis here, as there were in Conakry. We had to make
up our minds to walk. But we were back at my house
within less than half an hour. I went into my mother's
hut, followed by Konaté, still silent as ever. Ex-
hausted, I lay down on a mat. My gaze fell on the
portrait of my grandmother hanging on the wall. I
knew she was no longer alive, that she was in the land
of the dead. My mother had written to me in Paris
about her passing; and, without speaking about it to
anyone, I had spent over a month in bitter sadness.
Now, my gaze fell on that face which gazed back at me
too. It was as if my grandmother had been brought
back to life; her look became animated, as animated as
a look can be, and I heard the old lady telling me:
'Look after your little brothers and sisters. Be to them
as I was to you, an example of goodness and tenderness.'

Suddenly, my heart began to beat more quickly. I
felt distressed by the void left among my uncles at
Tindikan by the death of my grandmother, who had
been the pillar of the concession. Automatically I put
my hand on my heart, as if in the hope of calming its
violent beating. 'Grandmother is dead!' I kept telling
myself. Everyone carries his own death within him.
She had carried within her the death of one whose
goodness and love for her work had made her a great
woman.

Then I raised my gaze a little higher, to the roof of

the hut. It was sagging slightly; in places, the supporting beams were laid bare; daylight filtered through tiny holes and fell directly on the calabashes and plates laid out on the ground. Yet nothing could rob the hut of its simple nobility, which derived from its style of construction, from its circular walls of immaculate whiteness, painted with kaolin, from the perfect cleanliness of every nook and corner, from the ingenious fashion in which my mother had stacked the eating bowls, graded in order of size, on an old chest standing like a sideboard in an alcove. It did not matter that the roof was slightly sagging and in places riddled with holes: the nobility of the whole seemed all the more apparent.

While I lay there remembering my grandmother, a knock on the door interrupted my reverie. Marie looked in and announced:

'The meal is ready. It is served in our hut.'

I looked to the left. Konaté was sleeping. I shook him awake.

'Konaté, it is the hour of the midday repast.'

'That is good,' he said, standing up. 'I shall go back to my house.'

'Stay and keep us company.'

'No, Fatoman. I told the "Boss" I'd be back. She'd be angry with me.'

He took leave of me. I went out, followed by Marie. In the courtyard of our concession my mother was calling to my 'little mothers' and my sisters, inviting them to come to her hut for the noonday repast.

After the meal, I began wondering what kind of typical local craftwork I could find to take back to my friends in Paris. I was thinking now of what my father had told me: that he had been devoting himself entirely to sculpture ever since the women had started buying the junk imported by Lebanese and Syrian merchants.

I went to his workshop-studio. My father was busy

carving, surrounded by his apprentices. I sat down beside him and watched him shaping the wood. Mysteries
and miracles were being born under the keen blades of
his chisel and adze. With fascination I watched my
father rough-hew the wood; and I tried to imagine
what was going to emerge from the shapeless block on
which the blows of chisel and adze fell sharp and clear,
with an almost metallic sound, for he had started to
trim a piece of very hard wood. The work would take a
long time.

After fifteen minutes or so, the body of a hind began
to emerge from the wood. Yes, all of a sudden I
glimpsed a kind of outline in the wood, and I realized
that it would indeed be the figure of a hind that was to
issue forth from the lifeless block.

'My father,' I said. 'Might I have this hind?'

'Do you want it?'

'Yes, I should very much like to take it with me and
give it to one of my friends in Paris.'

'Very well,' he said, 'I shall give it especially careful
attention.' He lowered his head again and went on
trimming the wood. I watched his work closely. What
could my father be seeking as he carved and sculpted
the block? . . . Reality, perhaps! . . . He was seeking to
be true, as true as it is possible to be; he was seeking to
be as close to reality as it is possible to be. I could see
quite clearly that his concern, his sole concern, for
truth, for reality, in the performance of his work, was
tempered only by his search for an ideal beauty, and
consequently for the creation of a type of universal
beauty.

And indeed, after two hours' work, the shape which
had unexpectedly emerged or begun to emerge from
the wood became a beautiful hind, a very beautiful
hind; a hind, in fact, that expressed the essence of
every type of hind roaming our savannahs.

'In the museums of Paris, I have seen African sculptures but they are very different from yours. Don't you ever make any like that? The men who created those works were very cunning.'

'Very skillful!' he said. 'Everything you have seen like that, over there, was sculpted by our elders and betters, by craftsmen who had never been to school and who yet had more inborn talent and skill than we could ever imagine. One thing is quite certain: those men of the people, of the common people, had a power of contemplation and insight into creation much more highly developed than ours today, much closer to reality, much closer to truth. Each one of those anonymous artists whose works of genius now lie in museums had more genuine ability in their little finger than we, their descendants, have in our entire hands. I am well acquainted with those forms they produced, but I do not make them myself. They are rarely carved nowadays. Those forms date from a far-distant epoch, the time of our ancestral fathers. It was an epoch when the hind, emerging slowly from the wood under the tongue of the adze, served the cause of magic, served a cult. It was a time when the blacksmith-sculptor was a magician, was a wizard, was a priest, when he practiced more than a mere craft, because the nature of his art demanded that he work always in relation to fire—first, in the smelting of ore, and then in the working of metal. The weapon that was the work of his hands was a weapon that could wound, not just because it was sharp or skillfully handled, but because it had been imbued with the power to wound and to cut. The hoe of the peasant was not just a tool that turned the earth, but a magic talisman that controlled the soil and ordered the seed times and the harvests. In those days, the art of the blacksmith surpassed by far that of all other craftsmen: it was in all truth a noble art, a magician's art, a real art, indeed, which required more knowledge and more skill than the other arts. And so it

was natural that in those days it was to the blacksmith
one turned, not to sculpt a hind, something that anyone here can mock up, but to model the images of
one's ancestors (and the most remote image of all: the
totem), to carve the masks for ritual dances, to fashion
every cult object, which the blacksmith's inherent powers rendered sacramental by the very fact that it was he
who created them. Though such powers have never
entirely died out, my son, nevertheless I cannot conceal
from you the sad fact that they have more or less lost
their potency, and that it could hardly be otherwise
considering the essential nature of our society which,
although it did not break completely with its ancient
beliefs, all the same allowed itself to be converted to
Islam. If our caste is still a powerful caste, it seems to
be by virtue of the fact that we blacksmiths and metal-
workers are creating sculptures that are more and more
remote from any kind of religious preoccupation. And
it is not so much that the ideas of power and mystery
have died, have disappeared, as that the mystery and
the power are no longer to be found where they used to
be; for they are beginning to fade away under the
influence of modern ideas. That is why the hind you
are going to take with you will never be anything more
than an ornament, a decoration.'

'My father, you have spoken about your ancestors.
How did they go about making works so instinct with
natural rhythm, so alive with wit and grace?'

'Our ancestors,' he said, 'did not copy reality; they
transposed it. Sometimes they even transposed it so
much that there would creep into the image they were
creating, something abstract. But it was not a systematic abstraction; rather it is an abstraction that
appears to be a means of expression extended to its
utmost limits, yet uncertain of those limits. But our
ancestors did not usually approach their transpositions
of reality in such an objective and calculating way;

they allowed their hearts to speak more naturally; and so their transpositions led them to a distortion which first of all emphasizes and accentuates the expression, the spirituality of the object, and then, in turn, dictates other distortions, purely plastic this time, which balance the initial distortion and turn it into a work of art.'

'My father, what you teach me is fascinating. But you have just told me that the distortions were not gratuitous, that they were not just a trick, that they were in response to the artist's inner need, his desire to achieve a certain spiritual expressiveness . . .'

At that, he began to laugh, and went on laughing some time before making this reply:

'You're trying to tell me, my son,' he said, still laughing, 'that if these distortions were not just a trick, it is surprising that they should have been organized into a whole with such mastery? Well, that is what we mean by rhythm, the rhythm we feel also in the playing of our tom-tom artists; it is that inborn gift that used to inform, and even now still sometimes informs the souls and the hands of our craftsmen-artists.'

He stretched himself leisurely, then, after a luxurious yawn, took some glass paper with which he began to polish the hind; for now, his work was finished, well and truly finished. Meanwhile Bilali and Konaté had turned up. One after the other they took the carving of the hind in their hands and admired it. Then they expressed their desire to attend a political meeting.

My father put down his tools for a moment, set aside the glass paper, raised his eyes to heaven and said:

'May the Lord preserve you from the wiles of Satan!'

'*Aminâl*' we all replied.

'Fatomanl' cried my father, when I was already in the street with my friends.

'Yes, my father,' I replied, returning to the work-shop.

'Never forget that the insect is eaten by the frog, and the frog is eaten by the serpent.'

'I do not understand you, my father.'

'The insect,' he explained, 'is the rich man. The frog is the intellectual. And the serpent is the king.'

'You mean,' I hinted, 'that the leader is above all, above the rich man and the intellectual?'

'Yes, my son,' he answered.

'And what makes the leader fall from power, my father?'

'The thing that causes the leader to fall from power, even more than popular revolt, is *haké*, that is, the injustices he afflicts on his people.'

'Which signifies that the Lord supports the leader only when the latter shows himself to be a just and good man?'

'That is so, my son,' he gave answer.

'But who is he, this leader?'

'The leader is the vice-president of the government. From now on, he holds the country in his hands.'

'I understand, my father.'

'Go now, my son,' he said.

'*Au revoir.*'

'Until this evening, my little one. I wish to see you, my son, you and your wife, this evening in my hut.'

Party Meeting

AT THE PARTY MEETING, Konaté, Bilali and I encountered such a large and closely packed throng, most of them flowing over into the street, that we regretted not having come long before in order to get seats in the interior of the concession in which the meeting took place.

We were tempted to stay in the street, listening from that vantage point to the political perorations of the various speakers. But we plucked up our courage, and, elbowing our way, we insinuated ourselves into the mass, into the black wave of humanity. As good luck would have it, we succeeded in settling ourselves, not without difficulty, on the end of a bench close to the committee members. The setting sun, suspended above our heads, illuminated us with brutal clarity. The silence weighed upon us. Suddenly, one of the men at the main table snapped his fingers, indicating his desire to speak. He stood up at once. Clearing his throat, he began his speech in Malinké. I liked the look of this man. Our eyes, the eyes of all of us, were fixed only upon him.

'Comrades,' he began resolutely in a voice of bronze,

'we thank everyone for his labors and for the good will shown. I should like all those present to know that an enormous task has been fulfilled during what is now almost one year since our party, the great R.D.A.,* has been directing and controlling all the activities in our country. I should like all to know that if we press to with the same courage and the same perseverance, we shall see here in our town, Kouroussa, extraordinary changes.

'Comrades,' he went on, 'if we work as we ought to work, we shall transform our little town of five thousand inhabitants within a short space of time into a great modern city, into a remarkable metropolis. If we take good care of the trees we have been planting all along our streets, they will grow fast, very fast.'

I turned round and cast a quick glance at the audience. All seemed to be hanging upon the orator's lips. Indefatigably, he continued his peroration:

'By hard work,' he said, 'we shall construct houses of one, two and even three stories. In less than ten years, therefore, we can expect to see our city rising out of the trees. Yes, the edifices we shall have raised shall, thanks to our labors, raise their noble brows above the dense foliage that we shall see gaily flourishing tomorrow on the trees we have planted. From the topmost stories, we shall be able to see the Niger, our great River Djoliba! . . . All ye who now suffer from the heat and who betake yourselves every evening to refresh yourselves on the banks of the Niger will no longer need to make the trip: ye shall have the great river and its fresh airs in your own homes, ye shall enjoy these advantages high above the swelling waves of dense foliage. All ye who are here this night dream, I am convinced, of that great happiness and pleasure . . . This dream, that is no longer only a dream, has vigorous roots in reality, for, thanks to our labors, we

Rassemblement Démocratique Africain. (African Democratic Assembly)

have widened our streets, constructed bridges and built roads . . . Comrades, if we keep at it, there is no reason why we should not achieve the aims we have set ourselves. Comrades, I thank you.'

He sat down, greeted by a burst of applause. For several minutes, a confused buzz of talk and cries of joy could be heard. Then, when silence had once more been established, the second speaker took the stand:

'Comrades,' said he, drawing up his tall figure to its full height, 'I shall not give you a lengthy oration, not after the brilliant address which has just been given you by our illustrious member concerning one of the aspects of our Party's activities. The point I wish to take up, and on which I shall allow myself to give particular rein to my thoughts, is the concern we should all of us feel for the trees which we have just planted. And why have we planted them? Possibly because of the grateful shade they will cast and the picturesque appearance they will lend our native land in the years to come. But above all, we planted those trees so that they might bring us prosperity . . . Yes, comrades, prosperity, for the members of our committee, in planting those trees all over our town, have had in mind the Konkouré Project, the fulfillment of which, as ye all know, depends on reserves of water that are indispensable to the production of power for this our native land. Within a few years at the latest, the reforestation plan which our committee and other committees of the Party have put into action since the institution of self-government, will accumulate such vast quantities of water that we shall be able to draw upon their reserves as much as we like. Our Guinean prairies will ever be green, yea, despite the most crippling droughts. And lo, at no matter what period of the year we shall be able to cultivate, in well-watered paddy fields, the rice that is our staple food . . . These are some of the reasons why comrades from the surrounding villages should prevent forest fires, so as not to squander idly our economic potential. Moreover, these trees, planted all over our native land will bring benefits to neighboring peoples, and even beyond these to regions of Africa far removed from ours.'

The audience applauded lengthily. When everyone was silent again, the speaker went on:

'Comrades, I thank you!'

He gave a satisfied smile. Then, resuming his serious mien:

'Ye are by no means ignorant of the fact that the rivers Niger, Senegal and Gambia have their source in Guinea, in the Fouta-Djallon, and that consequently the prosperity of a certain number of countries depends, and will always depend, on the care we take of our forests, of the trees we have planted there. Even the climate of West Africa itself, whose reserves of water are to be found here in Guinea, could be mitigated also as a result of our efforts in this direction . . . Comrades, I thank you!'

Renewed, enthusiastic applause. The orator sat down again, confident that his contribution had been understood. Everyone approved of what he said, without one dissident voice. It was known that the other sections of the Party were discussing the same problems that day, and that by the following day and the day after that, these problems would be being talked over by the millions of Guinean inhabitants. Perhaps from now on the trees recently planted would no longer be neglected; perhaps no one among the thousands comprising the Party committees would ever again set fire, as had been done before, to the brush . . . That the very next day or the day after the convention the Party's Politburo would intervene, as a last resort, to codify the decisions taken by these thousands of committee members and make them law.

The word was then passed to another member of the

Bureau. An elegant young woman, with high, pointed breasts like a Peulh woman, with teeth of an immaculate whiteness like those of a Malinké woman, with the seductive bearing of a Soussou woman, and with a long neck encircled with rings like a woman of the forest zone—this woman whose physique, and whose character too, probably, represented all the women of the land, rose to her feet. From her first utterance: 'Long live the R.D.A.!' a sense of heroic grandeur invaded the audience; for now the sonorous reverberations of the words had more significance than their actual meaning. All with one voice repeated, in tones of vigorous conviction: 'Long live the R.D.A.!' The declining light of evening seemed to carry the voices very far; their echoes, returning to our listening ears, gave the assembly a more solemn and ceremonial character. But the woman who had spoken induced us to sit down again, for we had all leaped to our feet to shout: 'Long live the R.D.A.!' And thereupon she immediately began to speak:

'Comrades,' said she, 'I thank you from the bottom of my heart for having come here in such great numbers this evening to our weekly meeting. I am gratified to see among you a large proportion of young people. For our order of the day is an important one, and demands the undivided devotion of both old and young . . . I know that those who have come before me have spoken many things. But if I may impose upon your kindness, I should like to add a few words to those uttered by my comrades.

'We have already journeyed far on our long march since putting out of action the opposition party, since vanquishing it utterly and since our own beloved Party came into power in our native land. But how long, how infinitely long, is the path that still lies ahead, the road that still separates us from our final objective: the moral and material happiness of the whole of our people . . . Nevertheless, comrades, we are encouraged when we cast a fleeting glance behind us from time to time and behold all that has been achieved by our efforts since January 2, 1956, the date of our great Party's seizure of power . . . When we behold all that has been achieved by our efforts in every field, particularly in the domain of our children's education, the education of those very children who, on the morrow, in the glorious future that is to come, are to replace us as the leaders of their native land.'

The militant members of the Party burst into frenzied applause. She paused for a brief moment, a faint smile of appreciation wreathing her lovely lips. Then she went on:

'In those days when the B.A.G.* was in power our children had to cover incredible distances in order to go to school, because of the great lack of institutions of learning: when we remember this, how encouraging we find the work already carried out in this important field of education! Today, thanks to our Party's triumph and to your courage, thanks above all to our enterprising spirit, there are new schools in our region, new schools in all the villages of our region. On the morrow, comrades, all those schools, and the great mass of youthful minds that will thereby be politically orientated and engaged, and above all made full use of—all will work toward conditioning the development and the political force of Guinea, and by extension of the whole of Africa, and will impose upon our human society the wondrous image that we all are dreaming of.'

The audience, interested and carried away, applauded even more frienziedly. When the applause had died down, the woman went on, more quietly at first:

*B.A.G. *Bloc Africain de Guinée.* A neo-colonial conservative party. (*Translator's note*)

'Not so very long ago, there were very few Party cadres in Guinea—and we need many—because their formation depended upon the good will of the colonial power, which did everything it could to keep the majority of the people in a permanent state of analphabetism or semi-ignorance. Today'—here her voice rose again —'we are happy to realize that our town is also beginning to contribute effective working cadres in the service of our native land. Comrades, this night we have the honor and the joy to welcome among us one of our brothers, Fatoman, recently returned from Paris.'

Smiling, she indicated me with outflung palm; the audience gave me tremendous applause, and she had to raise her hands for silence in order to continue her speech:

'There is also the problem of peace. It would appear that certain men or certain nations cannot live in peace: these evil men want war. Now, if all the women on earth were to get together and decide on a general strike, of the kind that used to take place in former times, and which I shall call an "Anti-Man Strike," in one month—in one month only, comrades!—universal peace would be signed once and for all.'

A great howl of approval was heard. As one man, the entire throng leaped to its feet to shout:

'Bravo! Bravo! . . . Hear, hear! . . . Bravo! Bravo!'

'I think the meeting's over now,' Bilali murmured.

'I don't think so,' replied Konaté. 'Usually Keïta delivers the closing address.'

'What's his job?' I asked.

'I don't know, I really don't know,' replied Bilali. 'But he's very intelligent, and his speeches are always very instructive.'

Keïta did not keep us waiting long. As soon as we were all silent again, he rose, slowly, making the most of his short stature. He began to speak, 'ticking' his words, as we say in Guinea, because he was a stammerer.

'He's not very eloquent this evening,' Bilali exclaimed.

'He will be,' replied Konaté. 'But his speech never becomes interesting until after a certain time has passed, after the first few minutes, during which he stammers.'

'Stop talking, Konaté! Look and listen!' Bilali commanded.

Raising our eyes to the speaker, we felt convinced that Konaté's expectations would be answered.

'Comrades,' Keïta began, 'three of our comrades in turn have addressed you about important problems which interest all of us. I am sure from the start that we shall benefit from these instructive talks, and that we shall all, in our own best interests, put into practice what we have learned tonight.'

Applause.

'I thank you, comrades. After the seizure of power on January 2, 1956, we talked a great deal about equality. Now each one of us must give this word its true significance in his daily life. It is absolutely essential that within our committees and our trade unions there should always be true liberty of speech. However, in all places and at all times we are all expected, in duty bound—unless we want to see our society plunged into anarchy and thus made ridiculous—to respect the administrative hierarchy, which is nothing less than an extension of the power of the people. This respect must be shown in all places and at all times—in the places where we work, in our shipyards, in our offices, in our workshops—for our administrative heads have to make decisions dictated by necessity and by emergencies which are not always apparent on the executive level. These leaders possess information on the general trend of events which is often unknown to the rest of us. They also receive instructions from our secretary-general, who is at the same time mayor of Conakry and vice-president of the Government—and these instructions come from ministers and other high officials whom we, the people of Guinea, have elected to their exalted positions. We must therefore be disciplined . . .'

Once again, the crowd applauded. He continued:

'On the other hand, there are those of us who say that we belong to the South, or to the North, to the East or else to the West . . . Comrades, I'm telling you now, our movement, the great R.D.A., desires Franco-African fraternity and combats colonialism and its puppets, the instruments of that colonialism. I mean the reactionaries, the hired lackeys of the B.A.G. Respect these reactionaries (enemies of our great movement) as long as they keep quiet. But if they appear to be underestimating the strength and power of our Party, carry out your orders! That is: render saboteurs incapable of doing any damage, set fire to their huts. And then, properly admonished, they will never again attempt to disrupt the harmonious development of our native land.'

Renewed applause.

'Now there is one thing which it is always as well to stress,' he said, 'something that was always part of our main line of action, which was the key to our seizure of power from the reactionary party, the B.A.G., and to the eventual realization of our plans in every field of action. This thing allows us to overcome our enemies' foul machinations, and, in the years to come, will allow us to strangle at birth all other conspiracies and cabals which their saboteurs will inevitably hatch and harbor against us and against our Party. This thing, comrades, this extraordinary power, comrades, is work, justice, solidarity.'

The audience at these words was beside itself with joy. Rising to their feet, they applauded and shouted bravos of encouragement. The orator restored silence, then went on:

'It is not for nothing, comrades, that we speak to you always of work, of justice, of solidarity. These are authentic and fruitful slogans. Their value to our country is the same as that of the rails to a locomotive, of the brain to a man. Comrades, as long as we in our great Party of human emancipation make practical application of the real content of these words—work, justice, solidarity—our people's burning faith and patriotic zeal cannot but be strengthened as we march forward to fresh conquests and to the acquisition of ever-greater health and happiness. In this way, we shall reach very soon that glorious future of which my distinguished colleagues have spoken . . .'

Here his voice lowered to a threatening tone:

'But comrades, if we become sluggards and laggards, if we become unjust toward others and toward ourselves, the great leap forward taken by our Party, by the illustrious R.D.A., the Party of all Africans—yea, I say unto you, that burning faith and that great leap forward which our people have made shall wither away; and then our people will be tempted to adopt other attitudes—irrational attitudes such as despair, regionalism, tribalism and racism. Then shall the people be filled with great bitterness, and be turned against itself, against its own happiness. And then the least little push on the part of the traditional ex-leaders and of imperialistic neo-colonialism could cause our experiment to be stillborn.'

There was silence.

'Comrades, the first enemy of man is man himself. Our people carries within it always its own life and its own death. The death of each single one of us can be found in the hearts of each one of us here tonight. Therefore, comrades, let us overcome our faults, let us ever seek to become more pure and perfect, let us flourish with conviction the colors of our great Party, and let us hold fast to the key, let us hold that symbolic key with burning faith and boundless energy, the key of Work, Justice, Solidarity. It shall open unto us all the gates of happiness, to the glory of our common destiny and to the exaltation of our pride in this our great continent of Africa . . . We are against crooked deals, corruption and lies! We stand for unity and for the continual growth of democratization in our native land! We stand for true Franco-African fraternity! Long live the R.D.A.!' he shouted enthusiastically, with upraised arms.

Before him, the crowd yelled the same phrase.

'We shall ever be vigilant, comrades, in jealously guarding our great Party's achievements, that our children and our children's children may still feel, buried with us in our tombs, all this national pride that seizes our hearts and minds when we recall the glorious past of the heroes of Africa, they who fell upon the fields of battle and gave their lifeblood in the defense of African liberty! We stand for the rehabilitation of the black man, and for peace among all men on earth! Long live the R.D.A.!'

The crowd seized on this phrase, and yelled, more loudly than ever:

'Long live the R.D.A.!'

On the orders of the president of the meeting, the audience quietly dispersed.

'What do you think of this evening's meeting, Fatoman?' Konaté asked me when we were in the street.

Just at that moment I was watching one of our Malinké fays. She was just in front of us, walking along in a provocative manner. Bilali quickly asked:

'Do you fancy that one?'

'What?' I asked, pretending not to understand.

'That little beauty.'

My second native land?'

'Yes, that feminine beauty,' he elaborated, with a smile.

'She pleases me. But my mind is almost entirely occupied by my concern for my *first* love, my native land.'

In the sky, a plane's throbbing roar could be heard, taking off in the direction of Europe.

'Do you remember the day when you left us to go to Europe?'

'Yes,' I said. 'That's a long time ago now.'

'How many years?'

'I don't know. Perhaps as much as six years ago now.'

'When will you go back to Europe?'

'Soon, perhaps, in two or three days, with my help-mate, to whom I wish to show the marvels of Paris.'

'I notice *you* didn't make a speech,' said Bilali, 'even though our woman leader made a charming reference to your presence in the audience.'

'No, Bilali. I hate making speeches.'

'Nevertheless,' said Konaté, 'if you had been a member of the Guidance Committee, what sort of speech would you have made?'

'I don't know. All I know is that one day someone must attack all those lies. Someone must say that though colonialism, vilified by that committee, was an evil thing for our country, the regime you are now introducing will be a catastrophe whose evil consequences will be felt for decades. Someone must speak out and say that a regime built on spilt blood through the activities of incendiaries of huts and houses is nothing but a regime of anarchy and dictatorship, a regime based on violence. Someone must shout: "Long live liberty"; but it must not be forgotten that the deputy elected to the French Government by this country, and who has just voted at the Palais-Bourbon for the suppression of the Algerian freedom movement has acted like a neo-colonialist. At the same time, our closest neighbor, Senegal, governed by a deputy who is also a poet,* had taken a stand against the war in Algiers. *That's* what I call realism! . . . Someone must say that you have already betrayed the R.D.A. and, at the same time, the great humanist who was its founder. Someone must say that the violence you are now bringing into being in this land will be paid for by each one of you, and especially by the innocent. Above all, in order to establish a workable social system, there must be more concrete action, honest activity, and less speechifying; more respect for the opinions of others, more brotherly love.'

My friends left me. The meeting had lasted too long and the hour of the evening repast was at hand.

'Au revoir. See you tomorrow!' I called to them, before turning back, before penetrating the gloomy shadows of the mangrove trees.

Strangely enough, I had never until that evening felt and understood the divided nature of my being. My being, I now realized, was compounded of two inner 'me's': the first, closer to my own feeling for life, fashioned by my traditional animist background, faintly tinctured with Islamism and enriched by French culture, fought against the second, a personage who, out of love for his native land, was going to betray his true ideas by coming back to live in this new regime. A regime which would also, without any doubt whatsoever, betray at one and the same time, socialism, capitalism, and the African tradition. This kind of bastard regime now in process of formation, after using the Church, the Mosque and Fetishism for support, would, after its triumph, deny God. It had already destroyed

---

*Léopold Sedar Senghor. (*Translator's note*)

democracy after the advent of the '*loi Deferre*,' and begun to muzzle the innocent population of Guinea. In the future, it would transform our churches and our mosques into nightclubs, our sacred forests into places for theatrical spectacles. Thence arose the justified anger of Issa and of his brother the Prophet, demanding justice from the All High; thence arose, too, the lamentations that the virgin forests chanted to the gods. We were threatened by the vengeance of heaven. Thence the gradual degeneration of our native arts and social life, thence the frenzied brayings I had just had to listen to, and those madhouse screamings by which it was claimed we were constructing a society that asks only to eat and live in peace . . .

I had been walking straight ahead, and, without realizing it, had reached my home. The conflict between the two 'me's'—or rather, my helplessness in the conflict between these two 'me's'—was such that I could not eat. And so I went directly to my father's hut.

A few moments later, Marie rejoined me there.

'So you've come, Fatoman my son?' my father said on seeing me enter.

'Yes,' I said, laughing.

'And you, my daughter-in-law,' he said, looking at Marie, 'does your mother-in-law spoil you?'

'She is very sweet,' Marie replied.

'What did she give you?'

'Some golden earrings. And each of my sisters-in-law showered me with similar gifts. I am happy I came to Kouroussa.'

While this dialogue was proceeding, I was discreetly examining everything about me. It was six years since I had entered my father's hut, and I wanted to find out if the hut was still the same as the one I had left, the one I had known. Yes, it was still the same hut. In fact, from the place where I was now sitting, I could see out of a little window, the same little window which formerly always used to stand open, and through which I could see the stars glittering in the black firmament.

To the right, there was still the same bed of packed and trampled earth, furnished with a simple mat of woven osiers and a pillow stuffed with kapok. At the back of the hut, under the little window, there stood, just as before my departure for Europe, boxes of tools, and, to the left, prayer boubous and skins. Finally, at the head of the bed, hanging over the pillow and watching over my father's sleep, I saw a series of cooking pots. But this time, besides the cooking pots, there lay coiled among them a black snake: the very snake which I had been forbidden to kill* and which secretly I had cherished the hope of seeing that afternoon when I visited the workshop. I had not seen it there.

When Marie caught sight of the little black snake, she tried to run away. But my father prevented her and calmed her by saying:

'Fear not, my daughter-in-law. That snake will do you no harm.'

At a gesture from my father, a signal with his index finger, the snake began sliding toward us. Having reached my father's side, just beside the prayer skin on which he was seated, the snake rose upward on his tail, his body vertical and his jaws wide open.

'The snake says he is glad to receive your visit,' said my father.

After a little while, the snake coiled up again. His black body was shining with an extraordinary luster. Marie was afraid, very afraid; but she controlled her fear.

Then the serpent began to slip over the ground; he went as far as the wall, then swiftly slid over toward us again, opening his jaws wide.

'He says,' my father interpreted, 'that you shall go to

*See the author's *The Dark Child*. (*Translator's note*)

Paris alive, that you shall return alive and that you will find myself still alive on your return.'

Then giving a sudden switch to the conversation I came out with:

'This evening I attended a political rally of unusual violence.'

'Does that surprise you?'

'Yes.'

'During the last six years, we've grown accustomed to violence. Ever since your departure we've been treated incessantly to the same speeches, the same frenzies . . . It's unbelievable,' he added, 'but it's true. And now the hyenas are dissatisfied.'

'Are there hyenas in Kouroussa?' Marie asked anxiously.

'Yes, daughter-in-law mine, there are hyenas,' he said with his mischievous smile.

He came close to me and whispered in my ear. Unfortunately I could only hear a lot of indistinguishable hissings and splutterings that tickled my ear and filled me with a gentle euphoria.

'Did you understand, Fatoman?' he asked, with a satisfied air.

During this time, the snake had slithered softly away, returning to its little nook among the canaries. Marie, uneasy, was trying to make out what was going on.

'No,' I declared. 'I didn't understand a thing!'

'Then why did you laugh when I talked to you?'

'It tickled my earhole.'

Laughing at me, he drew me close to him, then said in a loud voice:

'How stupid you are, Fatoman!'

'Why?'

'The hyenas are—the toubabs.'

'And what are we Africans?'

'Apes,' he replied.

I burst out laughing, finding these images amusing. And he went on:

'Using this manner of talking, we can express ourselves freely, without bringing any trouble upon ourselves. Do you understand me now, Fatoman?'

'Yes, yes,' I said, deeply interested.

The close attention I gave him made him talkative, more talkative than usual.

'Now things are going better. But just before the self-determination business, everything was very difficult.'

After a brief moment of reflection, my father added:

'You knew nothing about it, or only theoretically, since you were not here. You were "on the sea." '*

We nodded our heads in an affirmative manner. He went on to explain:

'But back here at home, we went through that period, which was often tragic, lived all through it. Fighting, horrors! . . . You can't imagine what it was like. Not unless you'd actually been here!'

'Fighting between Guineans?'

'Yes,' he said. 'Bloody battles between political parties. On the one side there was the B.A.G. and, on the other, the R.D.A. Party.'

'And it was the R.D.A. that gained the victory?'

'Yes.'

'How did that come about?'

'That's something I can't answer, Fatoman. An illiterate old man like me cannot explain such things.'

'Then I'll do it,' Marie intervened. 'There were two reasons for the victory. The Guinean R.D.A. is directed by a leader, and strongly supported by women, children and workers. The Party succeeded in indoctrinating them by making them promises. They took it all as gospel.'

---

*'On the Sea' means 'in Europe.'

'So you think, Marie, that it was through the promises they gave that the Guinean section of the R.D.A.
won a victory over the B.A.G. Party?'

My father, highly interested, was listening.

'Of course!' she replied. 'At first there were the
promises. But there was also *l'Union française*, a rela-
tively recent idea. The term (but you already know
this) dates from the Constitution of 1946. It replaced
and abolished that of the *Empire français* which dated
from the Colonial Exhibition of 1931. The novelty, the
generosity, the revolutionary aspect of this new idea
prevented it from taking root as it should have done.
Now the realization of *l'Union française*, a realization
which concerns the State and our very existence, was
of prime importance if we wished to perpetuate that
state and bring all its citizens together in peace and
understanding. Naturally, the citizens of *l'Union française* belong to various ethnic groups.'

My father and I were looking at her: she had a lot
to say about *l'Union française*. But I only wanted to
know how the Guinean section of the R.D.A. had
triumphed over the B.A.G., and I brought her back to
this point.

'The R.D.A. triumph,' she said, 'can be partly explained by the rise of *l'Union française*'

'And so?'

'To return to my little lecture about the ethnic
groups, I was wanting to say that nothing has more
closely united these different ethnic groups of *l'Union
française* than their realization of their differences and
their similarities, and the compromise they worked out
between these differences and similarities. This is the
reason why, since 1946, large numbers of young Africans have gone to Paris. Sitting on the same benches
side by side with their white brothers, they tapped
knowledge at its true source. This is why, on a higher
level, the level of *l'Union française's* greatest responsi-

bilities, black, yellow and white leaders all sit together in the same Parisian assemblies. And you must not forget that the founder of R.D.A. is a Minister of State in Paris.'

'You mean to say that it is because of him that the Guinean section of R.D.A. has triumphed here?'

'Beyond a doubt. Without his prestige in Africa and in France, without his moral and material support, the R.D.A. in Guinea would have been beaten by the B.A.G., which had among its members more worthwhile men.'

'Yes, yes,' I said. 'I understand.'

'In plainer terms, on the hierarchical level, the governor of Conakry and the governor-general in Dakar are both dependent upon Paris. Through fear of disrupting the harmony of *l'Union française*, and also through fear of rousing the demagogues, the governor and governor-general kept quiet about certain activities carried out by members of the Guinean section of the R.D.A. Most often the administration did no more than summon them and tell them to behave themselves.'

'Oh, that must have been terrible!' I cried, very distressed. 'And naturally the tussle must have been organized with great skill.'

'Of course! The competition between the two political parties was very fierce. In a very subtle way, the Guinean section of the R.D.A. kept provoking the opposing party, and vice versa. Each time the dispute was precisely calculated by the party leaders so as to cause the maximum of disruption in their respective ranks: there were nightly burnings of huts, and often murders.'

'And what part did the hyenas play in this affair?' I asked.

'The hyenas had nothing to do with it,' said my father.

'I wonder what will be the future of this country, after listening to everything you have told me.'

'God alone knows what the future will bring,' my father said bitterly.

'You must have some idea. The black snake has already revealed the future to you,' I hinted.

My father smiled, as if caught in a trap. Then, with a defiant air, he stooped toward his bed of beaten earth, took the pillow and opened it with a little knife. From it he extracted a white ball encircled with cowrie shells and held it out to me.

'Here!' he said. 'Put that inside your pillowcase tonight and ask God yourself to enlighten you about the future of our native land.'

I took the ball.

'Now go to bed, both of you,' he ordered us gently. 'It's getting late.'

We went back to our hut. I slipped the ball under my pillow, and, a few seconds later, with the bedclothes wound tightly about us, we were sleeping like logs.

Dramouss

A MAN PROPORTIONED like a colossus, and so tall that I seemed, beside him, the tiniest of figures, was standing at the entrance to a house. This house, very dark, was surrounded by a circular wall. And this wall was so high that its top seemed to be lost in the heavens. Probably it was built this way only in order to compel the people it enclosed to leave only by the one gateway, where, standing with his great legs astride, stood this colossus with the hunched shoulders.

I went to take a look at the place. This was not difficult, for I only had to cross the road, a well-kept road, which separated the lofty wall from the hut in which I lived. But scarcely had I crossed the road, scarce had I arrived at the entrance to the high wall than the giant with the hunched shoulders grabbed me by the feet; then, whirling me around like a sling above his head, he flung me high into the sky. I stayed up there a while, floating on the passing clouds, for I had become light, yes, as light as kapok. But soon, regaining my weight, I began to fall. But too slowly. Looking down between my feet, I was horrified to discover, in a corner of the immense courtyard surrounded by the high wall, a lot of starved and ragged men, most of whom were writhing and screaming under the lashing whips of guards as big and strapping as the one who had flung me into the heavens. My slow fall finally brought me down to earth on the road, not far from the high wall.

'You're a prisoner,' I heard the giant with the hunched shoulders say to me.

'I know,' I replied, picking myself up and dusting down my boubou.

I crossed the road and the pavement; but, realizing that I had been caught in a trap, I was afraid, horribly afraid. And my body began to shiver as if with fever. I wanted to shout for help. Actually, I was opening my mouth wide, but no sound came out; the sound of my voice did not carry, could no longer make itself heard. Moreover, when I opened my mouth—and I opened it very wide in vain attempts to wrest some kind of shriek from my lungs—my jaws remained stuck. In order to close them again, to make them return to their normal position, I had to force them shut with my hands.

So I gave up trying to speak, and tried to run away. But I had barely taken three steps before the giant seized me by the shoulders and shoved me inside the high wall.

'You can't do a thing,' he said cynically. 'You are a prisoner.'

I looked at him closely. With his monstrous build, his knotted arm muscles, his hunched shoulders and his colossal power he would obviously give me a terrible pasting if I tried to run away again. 'No,' I told myself, 'one cannot escape when one is under the eyes of a man of that stature, of that breadth of shoulder. Better to try to overcome him some other way, by the force of argument rather than by brute strength.' And I began to speak, for I was no longer dumb; suddenly I

had regained my powers of speech. The flow of words
—strangely enough—was now so dense, so rapid, that
I could not control it completely.

'Will you shut up, you chatterbox!' he commanded.

'Very well. But do not shove me into your prison . . .
Let me go home.'

'Let you go home!' he yelled. 'You are too young. If
necessary, I shall drive into that head of yours with
hammer and chisel the realization that on this earth the
one law that counts (even if it is not the best law in
God's eyes) is the law of force.'

'Is that so? . . . Well, yes, here, that is true,' I
admitted, at a loss for words.

That gigantic, powerful man, who had already
shoved me inside the high wall, that monster, rather—
even if what he said was absurd, was it wise to contra-
dict him? . . . To throw words at him? 'Hardly wise,' I
thought to myself. 'All he needs to do is to raise his
hand (or rather, just his little finger) and he could
grind me into the earth.'

'Accept the fact that you are now a prisoner,' he
said ironically, adjusting his jacket and his bayonet.
'That's the best thing you can do.'

'I expect it is. But why are you throwing me into
prison?'

'I shall answer your question. But it'll be the last
one,' he snarled. 'You're getting on my nerves.'

He burst out laughing: a forced, mocking laugh,
then pulled a whistle out of his pocket, raised it to his
lips and blew on it three times. At this signal, all the
prisoners rapidly lined up in the courtyard in three
orderly rows. And when all had been lined up thus, the
giant pointed successively to the first, the second and
then the third row, shouting:

'First row: hard labor for life.'

'Second row: twenty years' imprisonment.'

'Third row: five years' imprisonment.'

'As for you,' he said, pointing me out to the others, 'you are condemned to death.'

'What? What?' I cried.

'What? What?' he mimicked me, with a roar of laughter.

'Yes, what! Why?'

'It was not I who condemned you to death,' he said.

'Then who? Who would do such a thing?'

'I tell you it wasn't me.'

'But who? Who would do such a thing?'

'I tell you it wasn't me.'

'But who? And why?' I shouted.

He looked me up and down, from head to foot and then from foot to head, always with his mocking look, as if he were laughing at me all the time. Then he snapped out, coldly:

'It was yourself. No one else. It is you who are condemning yourself to death.'

'Me?' I retorted, shocked.

'Yes, you yourself!'

'How can that be?' I murmured plaintively.

'You are like the *linké*,' he yelled, 'exactly like that gigantic tree which, instead of casting its shade at its feet, has the queer notion of extending it for miles around, abandoning its roots to the sun, even though they need humidity in order to keep the tree alive.'

'But! . . .' I ventured to break in.

'No!' he cried sternly. 'Let me speak. I know that when you see the very lowest of men, you become attached to him. And you even give him money, you express charitable feelings toward him. Even more, you consider him as a brother; as your elder brother or your younger brother. You are so naïve that you expect something of him. You expect gratitude from him. Only, by casting your shadow elsewhere, by depriving yourself for others, you are condemning yourself. So you have only yourself to blame.'

'Whatever I do for my fellow man I do also for myself and for God,' I replied.

'Instead of putting yourself at the service of others, you should put yourself at the service of yourself.'

'I put myself at my own service too.'

'Not at all!' he cried. 'You're just naïve, d'you hear me? . . . A dupe!'

'My credulity and my naïveté allow my conscience to rest in peace.'

'That's what is condemning you to death!' he yelled.

Then in a quieter voice, but nevertheless in reproachful tones, he went on:

'It's absurd to give ear to any Tom, Dick and Harry. Yes, whenever a man pays you a visit, tells you a lot of nonsense, piles one improbable story on another, you, without listening to the man more carefully, without pondering whether what he says is true, you shower him with your opinions and your money. The poverty of any passing stranger arouses your generosity, and you rob yourself to send him away happy.'

'That is how one comes close to God,' I hazarded. 'It cannot be done otherwise.'

But the word God seemed to offend him. He wrinkled his forehead (and disdainful lines appeared on it) and so appeared to be searching in his mind for a word, for the last word. Clearing his throat, he went on:

'In fact, you listen to yourself more than you listen to others. And you will always be a victim of your own good nature.'

'But what on earth are you trying to get at?'

He started a lengthy grumbling:

'Well, you see, you're dying by inches. Your naïveté, or rather the consequences of your naïveté will bring you inch by inch to your end. You should rather feel gratitude toward me for being cruel only to be kind, for condemning you only in order to correct your mistaken views on human beings and on God. After a stay with my prisoners you'll begin to understand things better.'

'You can do what you like. Your prison will never alter my essential way of thinking. I shall keep my convictions.'

'Does goodness ever pay? . . . Now, you have a heart of incredible gentleness and sensitivity! . . . The heart of a mother for her offspring! . . . It's a disgrace to have such a good heart. Goody-goody-goodness ruins a man.'

'What you call goody-goody-goodness is unlimited and uncalculated goodness. It enriches a man. That is the virtue God recommends and rewards.'

'God?' he cried again indignantly. 'But you're in the land of dreams, my poor chap! . . . On the contrary, it's the Devil who will pay you! I know you don't think much of me, but nevertheless allow me to give you this small piece of advice, until such time, of course, as prison shall have cured you completely of your illusions. When, out walking, you come across a fallen tree, you will do all you can to lift it up. If the fruit on this tree is edible, it will be of public benefit. And if it is not a fruit tree, its shade, the shade produced by its dense foliage, will be of public utility. But if, on the road, you encounter a man in difficulty, a sinking man, no sooner have you helped him to his feet than he gives you such a violent, barbarous and ungrateful kick that you are laid low forever.'

'I don't believe that.'

'I know,' he said. 'I know that you are behind the times. But you know perfectly well that, with time, you will come to agree with me . . . Well, that's that! Get back in line!' he ordered.

I returned to my prison. But when had it been constructed? . . . If the prison had been there the previous evening, I'd have noticed it as I was walking around;

and, dreamer that I am, I could not have failed to notice that high gray wall that rose very far into the heavens, which seemed to mingle with heaven itself. The whole thing seemed to be an immense continent. It wasn't a bad piece of work; in fact the architect who had conceived the plan had something like genius.

Unfortunately, police dogs, extraordinarily savage, roamed among the prisoners. It would have been better to send them elsewhere, for example to the commissioners of the municipal police, in order to allow us, who were already judged and condemned, to serve our time tranquilly in this lugubrious prison.

But what I could never manage to understand was the fact that they had imprisoned me. In this immense, mean universe, everything was known, the least word each man uttered was known to everyone, the slightest gestures commented by all. So it meant little to me that my presence here was noted and commented on. But my relatives, who had already suffered so much through me, would hear the news and feel such anxiety they would not be able to sleep at nights. I suspected one of my neighbors, with whom I did not get along very well, of giving me away to that brute of a guard. In my cell, I had taken off my caftan; I had folded it to make a pillow and had lain down, because it was late. I did not sleep; I did not want to sleep, preoccupied as I was by the loss of my liberty. Soon I could hear the hiss of whiplashes, the same as those I had heard from the sky when the guard had flung me up there and I had cast a glance down at the earth. In the end, I got up.

Who said that a prisoner did not have the right to sleep? Who said that I was not to be allowed to rest in peace that night? Obviously all the sounds were coming from the neighboring cell. Obviously it was my neighbor's turn to be flogged that night. What a stupid thing a prison is! When one is locked up (I do not mean when one locks oneself away) one realizes that liberty is a precious thing and that man should do everything to preserve and protect it. In a short while, I should attempt to escape; I should go far away; never should I be able to accustom myself to captivity. No man on earth willingly allows himself to be deprived of his freedom.

Even if all chance of escape were impossible, the desire to escape would still remain with him, to breathe the air of freedom, that air whose value is beyond price! . . . But the sounds of the whip were coming from the next cell; their loud reverberations never ceased. I simply had to go and see for myself.

I went to see for myself. I found the giant at the door of the next cell. There he stood, that brutal creature with the thick neck and hunched shoulders, just as I had seen him for the first time at the entrance gate; but this time he was adjusting his tunic and his bayonet, making use of his forearms; because he did not want to dirty himself, and his hands were crimson with blood.

'You again! What are you doing out at this hour?' he said on catching sight of me.

'It was those whiplashes, they seemed as if they would never stop . . .They disturbed me.'

'I've finished with him now,' he said. 'Tomorrow it'll be your turn.'

'Tomorrow?'

'Yes. You shall be corrected, flogged and whipped until the blood is drawn. So that when you take your leave of us you may be cured, definitely cured of your illusions!'

'Was it a prisoner you were flogging like that, until you drew blood?'

'Of course. You are given freedom, you are allowed to do whatsoever you wish in here, and you won't leave me in peace!'

I couldn't see that happening. I thought it more likely that this character would cut out our tongues and tell us to speak, cut off our feet and allow us to walk. These whiplashes cut out our tongues and that wall cut off our feet; we were brought down to the level of robots who have to bend in blind obedience to the will of their master. I have often seen prisoners, but never have I seen any who suffered so many privations as regards water and food, so many restrictions and so much corporal punishment.

And that's what he calls liberty! . . .

'Was it some very serious crime the man had committed?'

'Don't you know him?' he said, bursting into laughter. 'Until now I haven't been able to get a scrap of useful work out of him. He doesn't know how to sweep the floor; he doesn't even know how to take the rubbish bin and empty it on the trash heap. So far that prisoner has cost us more in food than the value of the services he has rendered. Even if, from tomorrow morning onward, he should show the best will in the world for the next three years that remain of his sentence, he would still be in debt to us and to our prison. Actually, for my part, I do not count on the slightest measure of good will from him. Instead I must count always on his mulish obstinacy. Since coming here he has done nothing for us.'

'Then why do you keep him?'

'Didn't I tell you he's a prisoner?'

'But if, as you say, he costs you more than the value of his services!'

'Even if he were to perform no services at all, and even if *we* had to be at his service, his sentence couldn't be annulled.'

He picked up a rag and wiped his red hands. I could see him looking at me from under his brows, as if trying to estimate what effect his words had had on my mind. But what effect could they have made? I no longer even believed that the three groups I had been introduced to on my arrival in this continent had been sentenced for some good reason. I now believed that the captives were there to satisfy the brute's own whims, so that he could impose his arbitrary system upon them, make them suffer under his sadistic rule so that he could look upon himself as a man of importance.

'Get back to your cell!' he told me suddenly.

Still wiping his bloody hands with the same piece of rag, he repeated: 'Tomorrow, yes, tomorrow it will be your turn.'

'My turn tomorrow?' I murmured sadly. 'All right. Well, good night. Please excuse me.'

'Excuse you—for what? And why?'

'I should not have gone on like this in the middle of the night, disturbing your rest and everything. But I just couldn't help it. Any restriction on my freedom of movement makes me talkative. And besides I had to find out where the sound of those whiplashes was coming from and who was suffering them. Who was suffering in such an ignominious way this deprivation of his liberty.'

'Tomorrow, when your turn comes, you will realize that here there is no such thing as rest.'

I went back into my cell and shut the door. The big brute must certainly be going back to his post at the gate. I lay down on the ground, on the damp earth, keeping on my caftan and rolling up my pipao as a pillow under my head. I closed my eyes for a while, about one hour; but I did not sleep; I was too afraid to fall asleep, too anxious to free myself, to liberate all the other prisoners. Again I heard groans coming from a distance. A prisoner was crying and moaning, some distance away . . . I left my cell again; I pricked up my ears in the direction from which the moanings seemed to come. They suddenly made me think of the sounds emitted by a man whose throat is being slit. Had the sadistic guard gone as far as to kill a prisoner?

'I say there!' I cried.

I could see him wiping his saber, red with blood, on a rag, the same rag he had used just now to wipe his hands.

'It's the tap in the washroom,' he said briskly. 'I'll go and turn it off. The prisoners, turning it on and off all the time have finally broken it, and now, each time the tap lets a little trickle of water run, it makes this curious row. At the present time, in fact, many taps have started emitting these strange moanings, really like goats bleating. Are you coming?'

I followed him against my will. I should have preferred to cast a glance into the cell from which these moanings were coming. I should have liked to see my prison companion and find out if it was actually that prisoner who was uttering these strangled moans, if it was the lash of the whip or the blade of the saber that was making the prisoner howl so. Certainly he must have been stuck by the saber. I could almost have sworn he had been wounded. I didn't believe in the tale about the washroom tap ...

Yet on the other hand I found it hard to admit that the giant would have dared to cut a prisoner's throat, a prisoner he simply had to guard . . . Nevertheless something told me that this beast would be capable of unimaginable cruelties.

But there he was in front of me, holding my hand; I did not have the courage, let alone the right, to resist, even a little, however much I may have wanted to. He had made up his mind that I should follow him; now he was escorting me.

Yet we did not go in the direction of the washroom. I might easily have confounded him by pointing out that a simple washroom tap could not possibly produce such moanings, but I was sick and tired. I was sick and tired of the sight of all those imprisoned people. I was sick and tired of looking at that brute with his hunched shoulders; I was sick and tired of breathing that air of animal brutality. Even the sight of him adjusting his tunic and bayonet with his hands or his forearms I had begun to find unbearable.

'Go back to bed,' he ordered me abruptly, as we arrived outside my door.

'Very well,' I murmured, terror-stricken.

I went back into my cell and closed the door behind me. A few minutes later, when I was quite certain he had again taken up his post at the main gate, I opened my door again and made my way toward the washroom. I wanted to prove to my own satisfaction that a tap cannot imitate the bleatings of a goat. Of course, I knew this already, but the big beast had so overwhelmed me with his flow of lies that I could not hope to be at peace with myself until I had tried to find out for myself. Just as I was going to open the washroom door, another prisoner caught sight of me. He called to me through the window grille in the door of his cell.

'Hey there! . . . Hey! . . . What are you doing roaming around like that?'

'I'm going to take a look at the washroom,' I replied.

'If the guard sees you . . .'

'Well?'

'He'll give you the flogging of your life.'

'Did the groans wake you up too?'

'Yes. Every night it's the same. He lets fly with the whip every night like that.'

'I'm not concerned with the whippings! Someone has been slaughtered in here, and, dying wretchedly and horribly, is moaning like a goat in the hands of the fetish doctor in the sacred grove.'

'Oh, that! The guard always ill-treats those who do

not come round to his way of thinking. And if you go on acting as you are now, you yourself are never likely to come up to his expectations.'

'Never come round to his way of thinking? . . . Is there a single man among all these prisoners who comes up to his expectations? We are guilty, we are all accomplices in these ignominies, since we accept them without complaint.'

'Without complaint?' he repeated. 'Don't forget that anyone who complains is immediately put to death. That's why everyone bears with this devil without complaint, without even a small complaint. That's why everyone is so afraid of the bullets and the knives, the cutting edge of the knives, the poisoned tip of the bayonets. Humanity at present is petrified with terror. Terror hangs threateningly above our heads. Terror peers through our eyes. Fear throbs in the ground beneath our feet. Terror watches at our doors, at the gates of our prison. Terror flows in our blood. Oh, how afraid we are, in this lugubrious dungeon! Afraid to walk in the courtyard, afraid of getting a bullet in the back, afraid of dying! . . .'

'Yes, but death would be welcome! . . . What about a hero's death? . . . Better to die than to submit for one single moment to imprisonment; than to accept, like schoolboys, detention in this terrible enclosure.'

'Don't you forget, don't you ever forget, that we are birds and that we are in the jungle, where strength is the only law. It is the most powerful law!'

'The most powerful, you think? I believe the opposite. *He* is only one, but *we* are thousands.'

'You're probably right. But the fear of death paralyzes us all.'

'All right, we'll talk about that later. If you are all paralyzed, I am far from being so. I'm going to look in the washroom.'

I left the washroom a few minutes later. The moanings of the washroom tap were sheer invention. The guard had deceived me. The deception was gross. I was convinced that a prisoner had been slaughtered.

And as I was so certain, I must set out to find the unfortunate man. I should try to bring him help. Could I let one of my fellow men go on groaning in agony like that? I thought for a moment. And then I decided to do something, and furtively crept into my neighbor's cell. I was horrified to find him stretched out on the damp floor . . . He was slowly dying, and in his painful agony was uttering frightful moans.

I went up to him and knelt at his feet . . . Then I noticed with horror that the throat had been cut, and that the head was attached to the trunk only by a thin strip of flesh, so thin that there appeared to be no hope. The man would never recover; he was already as good as dead. The body, lying in a pool of blood, was giving off a sickening odor. Revolted by this profanation of the breath of God, I went swiftly to my cell and decided to escape from this lugubrious prison before the break of day. That day on which, according to the giant, I in turn was to be flogged until they drew blood (or, indeed, until I was murdered), in the presence of a public who perhaps would raise no protest for fear of being massacred themselves.

Looking at one of the walls of my cell, I wanted to pierce through it in order to escape; but the wall was so thick and hard (it was of reinforced concrete) that even working with the best tools for several nights I should hardly have been able to get through. Even if the following day my execution was put off and I were to be left provisionally at liberty, I should never be able to escape. The high wall is stronger than frontier guards. In order to get out of this ergastulum and breathe the pure air on the other side of the wall, the air of liberty, there were such innumerable and complicated formalities to be gone through that even the most courageous and persevering of men would give up half-way. What we needed if we were to liberate ourselves was concerted action; we must all unite in one single thrust against the giant, and, uniting our thousands of wills, our thousands of arms, smash the horrible wall . . . In this dungeon from which I longed to escape I had no tools; there weren't any; not even a nail, a simple hook or any kind of metal object. Following the example of the sages, I decided to gather strength from meditation, so that God might send down his clemency upon me and on the host of prisoners. I prayed with such strength and conviction that it seemed to me God in person came and inhabited my soul. It seemed to me as if I had fainted away into God and that I no longer existed. Now it was his presence alone that illuminated my soul and my prison cell.

Radiant with joy, a joy that caused me to shed tears, I waited thus, on my knees, in the hope that something supernatural would free me and, along with me, all these imprisoned people. Finally day dawned. It grew light earlier than I had expected. When the cock crowed for the second time, two men dressed in black came to 'remove' me. We rapidly reached the courtyard, the immense prison courtyard, where a hundred soldiers, rifles to shoulders, and all on the same scale as the giant guard, surrounded a huge wood fire. No flame was to be seen, only smoke, a dense black smoke that poured upward and climbed very high in the heavens in tremendous spirals . . .

Not far from the soldiers there stood all the prisoners, earth-bound spectators.

I was carried into the center of the circle formed by the soldiers, to the very spot from which the dense, blackish spirals of smoke appeared to, or actually did belch forth. I wanted to scream for help, but the sound of my voice once more failed to carry. My anguish, and my longing to set myself free, to set all those prisoners free, had taken my breath away. I attempted to make a signal to the prisoners, hoping that, alerted by this sign, they would understand and lay hands on the giant and his armed companions. But as I gazed about me, dreamer that I was, I observed that I was completely surrounded by soldiers who were preparing to fire upon me. I was seized with terror, a dreadful terror . . . My body began to shake feverishly. But suddenly, strange to say, and in a fashion that even I could not explain, I saw myself in the sky. I had suddenly become a bird, a hawk which had flapped his wings and which, out of all danger, seemed to be hovering above the prison.

A few instants later, the guard joined me in my flight; he too had suddenly become a bird, but an astonishingly big bird, far more powerful than myself, the hawk. Hovering above me, he was preventing me from gaining height; slowly but surely he was forcing me down toward the inside of the prison.

When we had come down and were both inside the wall, not far from the roof of the cells, a great black snake appeared in the sky. It was swimming through the air very rapidly. It swam up to me.

'Quick, catch hold of me!' he cried. 'I have come to save you!'

I caught hold of him by the neck, and in a flash his body had described a half-circle and escaped from the menace of the terrible wall.

The snake rose into the sky like a rocket, so fast that the force of the wind pushed me flat against the back of the 'snake-rocket'; as long as he continued his extraordinary ascent it would not be possible for me to disengage myself from his scaly skin.

In that moment of deliverance and salvation, I turned my head and cast a mocking glance down to earth, to the prison. There was no more smoke; it had given way to flames which, seen from the sky, looked like a great glowing spot. As for the soldiers, they were scarcely visible; but I could hear distinctly the detonations of their rifles.

I spoke into the snake's ear:

'Did you see that down there?'

'Yes. The great conflagration, the bangs of the rifles. Don't you know what it means?'

'No,' I answered, hoping he would go on.

'It means you are saved, that they will abandon the plot they have been concocting against you. That the intrigues are over. And that you must remain good and keep your confidence in man . . . That's what life is! Anything else is slow death.'

'You mean the smoke is the symbol of evil, of machinations and obscure forces?'

'Yes,' he said. 'That's it exactly. But the flame you see below and the reports of rifles you hear are the symbols of defeat: the defeat of intrigues and schemings. It is simply,' he added, 'an expression of homage to your spirit of justice and feelings of solidarity with your fellow man. If you had accepted the giant's point of view, I should not have saved you.'

We were now beyond the reach of the machine guns and rifles, and also of the fire of wood, for now we were leaving the celestial vault and coming down to earth in a neighboring territory. I was yelling loudly, very loudly, not for fear of the bullets which could no longer reach us, or of the flames that could no longer burn us, but because our descent was rapid, was violent . . .

Despite this rapidity and violence, we finally landed without damage to myself or to the snake. The latter was even more glad than I was to be back on terra firma again and to have saved my life.

It was dark. Before me there appeared, not a great black snake, but a beautiful woman, extraordinarily

beautiful, whose hair covered her shoulders and back
and reached down to her heels.

'My name is Dramouss!' she said.

I did not reply.

A flash of lightning rent the universe . . . When I
had recovered from its dazzlement, I raised my eyes and
saw that the beautiful woman had disappeared. Doubtless the lightning flash had abducted her. Or perhaps
she had disappeared with the lightning flash, perhaps
even inside the flash itself. I did not know where to go.
After wandering around a bit, I finally recognized the
village where I had come down to earth: Samakoro. It
was many moons since I had last seen this village.
Samakoro was still the same as ever, dominating the
river, that River Djoliba which has its source in this
very region and which flows, swelling as it goes, on and
on, to lose itself finally in the far-distant ocean . . .

Yet everything was somewhat different from all I
had formerly known. It was Samakoro, but the men
and women living there were less numerous than when
I had left the place . . . Many of them must have run
away to escape persecution and famine. After all, did
not Samakoro now form an integral part of the 'Big
Brute's' domains? And did not the Big Brute amuse
himself by starving and terrorizing his subjects? . . .

So that is probably why, in this large village, the
straw huts were not crowded together as numerously as
in the past; they were no longer jammed up close
against one another; it was now a half-abandoned village. Where had the inhabitants gone? They must certainly have departed for distant but more peaceful and
prosperous lands and villages.

I kept on walking and wandering and walking, and
soon I realized that the lane I was walking along was
not the one I had known in former times.

It now seemed to me broader, better lighted. However, gazing all around me, I noticed, dreamer that I

was, that no storm lanterns were lit. Nor was there anyone walking about the streets and lanes. I kept on walking and walking, but I could not recognize the village, I could no longer recognize the lanes; these were not the straw huts that once I had known. And yet I was certainly in Samakoro! What was happening? What was happening to me? I do not know. I did not despair, but kept on walking. But however far I walked, however often I raised my gaze to scrutinize the straw huts, I could not recognize any of the lanes or the houses. So I decided to wait, concealed at the foot of a big tree, a cailcedra, for someone to come by who would lead me back to my house, or, failing that, to wait for the break of a new day. I waited a long time, several hours, for there were no passers-by. Suddenly I lifted my eyes to the heavens. To my great surprise and to my great horror, I saw, approaching with giant steps, a white shape which towered high into the air and seemed to be swathed in a white shroud. As the shape approached, I was able to make out a vague human shape. And that human shape was too queer, too queerly made, too tall, for me not to take fright. Nevertheless, I conquered my fear and called very loudly:

'Who's that? . . . Who's that? . . . Answer me!'

But did I actually call out? No sound came from my mouth. Terror had me by the throat. I had only imagined I was shouting. When I started again, I did not even have, as I did on previous occasions, the impression that I had uttered a sound; I was struck dumb. I closed my eyes. When I opened them again, I realized that I was standing under the great cailcedra, with the white silhouette confronting me. All round me, I discovered, piled at the foot of the enormous tree, there were corpses, numerous corpses. I was stupefied.

'Who is it? . . . Who's there? . . .' I repeated, in a voice that was choked with fear.

'My name is Dramouss. Do you not recognize me?' the shape demanded in an imperious voice.

She added:

'One corpse is missing. Go and pick it up at the end of the lane and put it with the others instead of standing there dreaming.'

I obeyed mechanically and went to the end of the lane where the corpse, or what the white shape called a corpse, was lying flat on its face. There, examining the face and trying to feel the pulse, I suddenly felt that the being lying in the lane was only asleep; it was not a corpse, not a corpse at all! This could be seen, I thought, from the plumpness of the cheeks and the dazzling cleanliness of the body. I decided to let the sleeper lie and went back. But at the foot of the giant tree, at the foot of the enormous cailcedra, the white shape had gone; that white form which towered high into the heavens, which seemed to mingle with the heavens themselves, was there no longer, but a giant woman with delicate features, light skin, a beauty of incomparable loveliness, and whose hair, extraordinarily long, covered her shoulders and back and came right down to her heels.

'It is Dramouss again,' the giant woman said. 'For the last time, I give my orders . . .'

'But . . . He isn't dead! . . . It's someone sleeping!' I babbled.

'No!' retorted Dramouss. 'It's someone who died in the "revolution." '

'What "revolution?" '

'Your revolution.'

'All right!' I answered resignedly.

Once more I ran to the end of the lane, my soul tortured like the flame of a torch in the wind, obedient to I no longer knew what impulse, and prepared to carry out this lowly task that the beautiful woman did not wish to soil her hands with. I took hold of the sleeper, trying to make him stand upright; but the rigid body, stiff with the stiffness of a corpse, heavy as lead, nearly made me fall over backward. Then I knew that it was a corpse . . . I decided to put it over my shoulder to carry it way. But the corpse came to life, got up and, like a flash of lightning, vanished . . . It had all happened as if I myself had been the resuscitated corpse, the reanimated dead man. Conscious of this sad fact, I took fright. Anguish spread through my whole being, that shook with fever.

'My God!' I cried in horror, raising my arms to the heavens. As I repeated my prayer, I felt my feet grow icy-cold, as if the ground had been inundated with icy water. When I lowered my head, I saw, with a fresh surge of terror, that the ground actually had been suddenly inundated. Who could have carried out such a perilous task so swiftly? I did not know . . . I ran away . . .

A few moments later, I found myself hidden in the foliage at the heart of the great cailcedra, and caught between two torrents; the immense torrent which had already flooded the ground and the lane and which was threatening to sweep away the branch to which I was clinging; and the torrent that had followed me step by step while I was climbing the enormous cailcedra. I had no other choice but to cast myself into one or the other of these two torrents, these two oceans; indeed, they were both the same and were on the point of joining. Placed as I was, I could neither advance nor retreat. Yet I continued struggling, against all hope; I struggled and strove, but my struggle was in vain. I was shouting, but no sound issued forth. And the water, that immense ocean, meanwhile, was there, rising and rising. The water was over my feet, the water was creeping along my heels; it was reaching my calves. It was rising very quickly, sure of its power. Then, while I was struggling and trying desperately to unclasp the

choking grip on my throat, I suddenly saw, looped
round the branch, a big black snake, its jaws wide
open, its forked tongue darting about inside. I plunged
my head beneath the water, in order not to have to see
the black monster. When I brought my head up again,
I found in place of the black monster the beautiful
woman whose hair, inordinately long, covered her
shoulders and back and reached down to her heels.
How had this metamorphosis been effected so suddenly? To that question I could really find no reply . . .

'I'm afraid! . . . I'm afraid!' I whispered, shaking all
over.

'Afraid?' she asked.

'Yes! Very afraid!'

'Of whom, and why? . . . It's just me again, Dramouss.'

'All right,' I said, resigning myself.

In desperation, I lifted my eyes to the heavens. Flut-
tering its wings in a sign of welcome, a swallow was
flying above the half-submerged branch; it swerved
with astonishing ease, almost touching my shoulder,
and seemed to be going to plunge into the flood. I
lowered my gaze, and met that of Dramouss, still
standing beside me, but this time with an enigmatic
smile wreathing her lips. She bowed her head, as if
better to view the rising waters, then raised her eyes
again at once. I then saw that her look was no longer
the same: her tender smile, too, had grown savage.
And, curiously enough, her eyes had changed! They
now resembled locomotive headlights, exceptionally
strong and luminous. She raised them to the dark and
lugubrious sky. And those two shafts of light carried
far into the heavens. On the verge of the infinite, of
unsoundable space, I then perceived, illuminated by the
headlamps of the beautiful woman, a multitude of
human beings who formed two long lines on an immense esplanade. From where I was, I could catch the
tumult of that crowd, though deadened, of course, and

weakened by distance and by terrible crashes of thunder.

The first line, that on the left, in flaming boubous, boubous on fire, were shouting despairingly; those in the second line, the one on the right, were clothed in sky-blue boubous and singing joyfully. At a point in between these two lines, an enormous blackboard carried the following inscription:

'ON THIS EARTH, MAN DOES NOTHING FOR ANYONE, NOR DOES HE DO ANYTHING AGAINST ANYONE; HE DOES EVERYTHING FOR HIMSELF AND EVERYTHING AGAINST HIMSELF.'

When the beautiful woman lowered her head again and focused her two headlamps on me, I fainted. But she picked me up at once; she brought me back to consciousness. And as I was standing up on legs still shaking with fear, my body still running with water, she began to speak again:

'Everything is swallowed up by the "revolution!" '

'The "revolution?" ' I exclaimed.

'Your "revolution," ' she said, 'is like this ocean of water that swallows up everything, annihilates everything.'

'What is to be done, now?'

'I was only able to rescue a rod of gold.'

'What rod?'

'The symbol of command,' she replied solemnly. 'As for the rifle, the *daba* and the assegai, rescued by me long ago from the hands of the "Big Brute," I am going to entrust them to the Black Lion.'

'What Black Lion?'

'The heroic Black Lion. He will preserve them a long time, for he is just, human and wise.'

I took the rod of gold. Before slipping it in my pocket, I noticed that it was a propelling pencil.

'Now, behold!' the woman suddenly cried.

'Behold what?' I asked, struggling against the flood-water which had by now reached my hips.

Raising my eyes, I saw something extraordinary: the moon was coming loose in the sky; then, when it had finished its prodigious descent and was resting on the ocean, it began to sail in the direction of the branch, already half-submerged, to which I was clinging. I stopped struggling to gaze at the sun above my head, and, on the ocean, the moon, which was still sailing in my direction. When it was quite close, I noticed that it was joined to the sun by a rope; I got aboard the moon which all at once began to climb toward the sun. Just as I was sitting down on a bench inside the moon, I had cast a quizzical glance through the porthole. There were no more huts, no more lanes, no more trees, no more immense cailcedra. Above it all there lay now only an immense expanse of water covering the entire universe . . .

Our ascent continued. When I cast my eyes about the place I was in, I found once more, on my right, Dramouss: that extraordinarily beautiful woman whose locks, this time scattered with starry diamond-flowers, sparkled like the Milky Way.

'Now,' she said, 'look straight ahead of you.'

I obeyed her, and then, to my stupefaction, saw the Black Lion, whose mane, the color of fire, covered all his visage. He was holding between his fore-paws the assegai, the rifle and the *daba*.

'Henceforward he shall be your guide!' cried Dramouss.

The Black Lion did not roar; on the contrary, he was very quiet for a lion. He took part in our games and pleasantries. He only roared and got nasty when one of us approached the rope connecting our bark with the sun. At that moment, fearing that one of us, either through stupidity or deliberately, might cut that rope (our craft would then have been swallowed up by the ocean and the moon would have sunk) the animal grew angry and growled fearfully. Apart from such incidents (as I have already said) he conducted himself very nicely, like an affable and courteous creature.

We were still ascending. And already the bells had sounded in the cathedrals, in the churches; the muezzin had continued calling the faithful to prayer; for the mosques, too, had been re-opened. The sacred forests, the plundered property, were restored to their owners; famine gave way to prosperity, illegality to legality, barbarism to civilization. And life, which had formerly been for us a mixture of sadness, absurdity and anguish, had once more become a thing of joy and laughter.

We were still climbing. As we ascended and the distance separating us from the flood and the abyss increased, our craft—that moon which, at the start, had appeared no bigger than a tiny hut—now attained the dimensions of a real planet. At that moment, gazing about me, I could see, I could recognize quite distinctly in the moon my Lower Guinea, my Middle Guinea and my native Upper Guinea. I could make out my Guinea of the forest regions, formerly persecuted and terrorized by the 'Big Brute.' I saw that they were profoundly and completely happy.

Yes, I recognized those girls clothed in *témourés* and iridescent loincloths, those young and old men, those young and old women. I gazed upon my Guinea guided with wisdom by the Black Lion, the heroic and wise Black Lion.

And I discovered that he was not alone: I saw that the host of his brothers was accompanying him in his marvelous ascent toward the sun; and toward that extraordinary source of light, toward progress; all embarked on the same ship, passengers responsible for one another, and destined for the same harbor. . . .

Fire

THEN I OPENED MY EYES and realized I had been dreaming. My hair was singed and my forehead bleeding: the thatched roof of the hut I had been sleeping in was on fire! Leaping up with pain as much as with despair, my eyes trying vainly to pierce the dense, blackish, spiraling smoke clouds, I jumped out of bed.

Fumbling and stumbling, I groped my way from one corner of the hut to the other. The tumult of flames was devouring the bamboo framework of the roof. Barely had it burned away than it all fell with a loud crash; in falling, the flaming wood caught the curtain and the mosquito net fixed to the wall. They in their turn caught fire, transforming my home into a furnace.

Still dashing desperately from corner to corner, I began to hear cries ... I could hear distinctly the voice of Marie, shrilly calling for help. I could hear the dull thuds made by the would-be rescuers who, using thick beams as battering-rams, were trying to break down the safety exit. For the main entrance, giving on the concession, was a mass of flames, and therefore unusa-

ble. Suddenly I was lifted from the ground, my arms
and feet were grabbed by two sturdy men; all at once,
the fresh air outside, reviving me, contrasted strongly
with the suffocating smoke-laden atmosphere inside the
burning hut. The fresh air seemed to lash my face and
body, slapping me back into life little by little. When
once again I could see the stars sparkling in the celestial dome, I realized that I was saved . . . Having
recovered from my initial fright, I saw that everyone
was hard at work in the back yard.

Wakened from sleep, our neighbors were there, some
of them naked from the waist up, others with loincloth
knotted round their necks, others still in *bila*.* People
who were usually neatly arrayed and 'clean as a new
pin' were now half-naked as they battled Satan's evil
agency. One might have thought it was the hour of
the bath. It was comical as well as tragic.

Obviously the shouts had been so alarming and
urgent that they had given no one time to clothe himself decently. At present the men were throwing water
over the flaming roof, which the women were bringing
in a variety of bowls, basins and calabashes.

This team of fire fighters drummed up for the occa-
sion played its part so well that it had the flames under
control before the arrival of the actual fire brigade. So
the conflagration's field of activity, which might have
extended to several other huts and even several other
concessions, was limited, thanks to the cooperation of
the neighbours.

'Fatoman! How did it happen? How do you account
for it?' my father demanded.

I was expecting those questions. I knew that someone would have to ask them. Nevertheless, on hearing
them, it was as if a thunderbolt had dropped on my

*Malinké word meaning 'pants.' (*Translator's note*)

head. Filled with shame, I muttered a few broken
words and fell silent. My mother intervened:

'Fatoman! Tell us! You're not a woman, after all,
you can't stay silent like that!'

'A woman?' my father quizzed her. 'But a woman
talks and talks! As far as words are concerned, no one
can surpass the women on this earth. You should
rather say that he is not a child any longer.'

I made up my mind. I had to defend myself, offer
plausible explanations and justifications.

'I don't know what happened, my father.' I spoke
timidly, in a low voice. 'I was sound asleep.'

He looked at me skeptically and a bitter smile played
round his mouth. This reply did not convince him.

'I had forgotten you are a smoker,' he said. 'It's one
of those bad habits you contracted over there. Perhaps
you dropped a cigarette end on the floor?'

'Perhaps. But I don't think so. Because in that case
the fire would have broken out earlier.'

'Not necessarily,' broke in my mother. 'It takes a
cigarette some time before it can set light to an in-
flammable object.

At that moment, Marie entered my father's hut. Had
she sensed my despondency? Women generally are better at guessing these things than men. Was she going to
save me? At once she began taking part in the discussion:

'It's very odd how it happened, father-in-law!' she
exclaimed. 'We spent a good part of the night talking
in your hut. Worn out, I fell asleep at once. But not
Fatoman. All night he was digging his elbow into my
side: I think he must have been having nightmares.
And toward five o'clock I woke up. There were flames
all over the roof of our hut! . . . Naturally, I shouted:
"Fatoman! Fatoman! Fire! Fire!" He half woke up and
told me, drowsily: "Lie down, Marie, you're dreaming." I shook him hard, but then, seeing he did not

wake up, I jumped out of bed, dashed through the main door, already in flames, and shouted for all I was worth: "Fire! Help! Fire!"'

'That's awful,' my father murmured, looking embarrassed. 'Did you both spend the night in the same bed?' he asked me softly, stressing each word.

'Yes.'

'You should not have done so! I forgot to tell you. When I gave you the "white ball" I forgot to tell you that you should sleep on your own, that you should not sleep with your wife.'

'You gave him that ball?' my mother asked in a strangled voice.

'Yes,' my father replied. 'Your son was asking questions. He wanted to see the Guinea of the future.'

'But he's not old enough!' my mother objected. 'He's not forty years old yet, the poor little lamb!'

'It would have been all right if he had spent the night alone.'

'How's that?' I asked uneasily.

'Dramouss, jealous of your wife, set fire to the hut. Have you the ball?'

'Yes.'

I went and got the ball and gave it to him.

'Ah, yes!' he said. 'Women are always jealous. Dramouss, jealous of your wife, set fire to your hut. It's my fault. It slipped my mind.'

Then my mother gave my father a severe look and told him roundly:

'Don't you go initiating Fatoman into your mysteries! He cannot understand. He's a toubab!'

'What's that got to do with it?' objected my father, shrugging off her reproaches and turning to me: 'But I expect you did have a dream, all the same, my son?'

'Yes, my father.'

'What did you dream, my son?'

'Frightful things, my father. I saw a people in rags

and tatters, a people starving to death, a people who lived in an immense courtyard surrounded by a high wall, a wall as high as the sky. In that prison, force was the only law; or rather I should say, there was no law at all. The people were punished and sentenced without trial. It was terrible, because those people were the people of Guinea, the people of Africa!'

'*Koun Faya Koun!*'* he exclaimed.

'But I also dreamed of a Lion, a great Black Lion, who saved us, who brought back prosperity to us, and who made all peoples his friends.'

'*Koun Faya Koun,*' he repeated. 'All that you have seen in your dream this night, my son, you shall behold upon your return to this country.'

Having slipped the ball back under his pillow, he stood up, opened an ancient chest and took out a wand of gold which he handed to Marie as he sat down.

'Here,' he said. 'This is some compensation for the possessions you have lost in the catastrophe.'

'Nothing was destroyed,' replied Marie, smiling, 'except the mosquito net, the curtains and the bedclothes, and they did not belong to us. All our things are in store at my mother-in-law's hut.'

'Take this gold all the same. Let it be your wedding gift from me. I am glad that my son has married you and that you came to see me. And so my blessings will go with you whithersoever ye go.'

We took our leave of him and were settled into a new hut. I was told that my father's apprentices would have the job of reconstructing the ruined hut.

During the two following days, my mother spent her time carefully packing our luggage. She did not forget to put in the carving: the statue of the hind which my father had presented to me.

We were shown every kindness. It came from older

*'It is the will of the All-High.'

people, most of whom had known me since I was a newborn baby, from my friends, from all my schoolmates, and particularly from Bilali and Konaté. We had been happy there in Kouroussa, and it had been no passing happiness. This and this alone is the image I wish to preserve in my memory, as well as the sad impression left upon me after my fantastic dream, in which I saw my country and its future. And already, before leaving Guinea, I knew that the grandiose communal plan which has been put into action was compromised in my compatriots' hearts because men had brought in doctrines which people were just swallowing wholesale, like coconut milk.

Finally the day came for our departure. The train drew into the station. Konaté, Bilali and my relatives had all accompanied us there. The station was crammed with people who, as a spontaneous gesture, had come to the station to demonstrate their friendship for me and for my wife.

'*Au revoir! Au revoir!*' we cried, as the train began to move.

They were all waving their hands. The women were also waving their brilliant silken scarves.

Then the next day we arrived in Paris. That Paris which for me was no longer, as formerly, a city of mysteries. . . .

Return

A FEW YEARS LATER, when Marie and I, surrounded by our children, found ourselves once more on the soil of Guinea, we took the train to Kouroussa as soon as our plane touched down. There we met my father, much aged. He greeted us on the veranda of his hut, with a smile which seemed to mock us gently, and said:

'The moment has come.'

My mother had come running and was already carrying on her back the smallest of our children. Not far from our concession a flag was flying in front of a fine modern building with simple lines. It was a red, yellow and green flag.

'What moment, my father?' I asked, pretending not to understand.

'The moment decreed by Dramouss,' he replied with the same mocking smile.

'Is Konaté here?' I asked, shying away from his allusion.

My father, lowering his eyes, said in an embarrassed tone of voice:

'Your friend was accused of being involved in the recent conspiracy.'

'What conspiracy?' I asked in stupefaction.

Marie and my mother listened to our conversation without taking part in it. Already my children, excepting the little one on my mother's back, were playing with my little brothers. Children are never strangers to one another.

'Konaté,' my father stammered, overcome, 'Konaté is no longer in the land of the living. Konaté was shot by the authorities.'

On hearing that, I burst into tears. My soul was deeply troubled, and my heart was desolated. My head swam with a great surge of protest, and my eyes swam with tears.

'But my father,' I said, drying my eyes, 'what about Bilali? . . . Is Bilali still here?'

My father ground his teeth. Again he looked at me, then lowered his eyes and turned away his head, saying:

'He too was a victim of the conspiracy.'

We remained seated in silence for a while, our hearts flooded by the heavy rains of our distress and sadness. After saying a few words of consolation, my father went on:

'Since your departure, many of your friends have been slain. Many people are in prison. Many others have fled, to Senegal, to the Ivory Coast, to Liberia, to Sierra Leone and other neighboring lands.'

He was silent. We remained thoughtful for a while. 'Why have I come back?' I wondered to myself. 'I too shall be slaughtered like the others.'

In the courtyard of the concession a mother hen, cackling with a grumbling note, her feathers all ruffled, was stepping out in a leisurely fashion, attended by her brood. Suddenly, out of the blue, a hawk which had been hovering above us for a moment plunged down on the concession. It flashed before our eyes only for a few seconds. When it swooped back into the sky we

saw, to our dismay, that one of the chicks was clutched
in its talons. The little chick was giving tiny peepings,
the sound of which reached us only faintly, as if stifled
by distance and by the predatory claws of the hawk.

'No, no!' my father cried, with a gesture of protest.
'Our regime puts our children before a firing squad for
the slightest thing. And that accursed hawk makes off
with my fowls, when there's no longer any food or
even a grain of rice left in the country!'

In a great upsurge of anger, but an anger more on
the inside than on the surface (as I could see from his
face), my father furtively plunged his hand into the
pocket of his caftan. He brought out a string of beads
which he brandished in the direction of the soaring
hawk. The bird of prey had now gained height and
would soon settle on the crest of the silk-cotton tree to
devour its victim at leisure.

'*Sala moûne gawlan mine Rabine Rahimine, adjib ly
yâ* Kachafa *ya ilou, Wal Djini Alga Atou Bintou
Maïmouna*'* My father uttered these words distinctly,
one by one, each time a pearl in the chaplet passed
through his fingers. He was seated, quite absorbed in
his prayers, and we sat watching him, anxiously, wondering what would happen next.

Suddenly, even before he had finished telling his
beads, the hawk, as if summoned (more precisely, as if
attracted by a magnet), swooped down to ground level,
beat its wings, then, gliding a moment as if trying to
regain height, suddenly came down to earth within
reach of my father's hand. The latter hastily pocketed
his string of beads, grabbed the hawk and wrenched
the chicken out of its talons. Then he picked up a
bulrush—there are always some lying about our con-

---

*'God, I call upon thee through the intermediary of Bintou, daughter
of the Djinn Maïmouna and through his master the Rouhania Yâ
Kachafa Ya ilou.' The presence of the genie 'Rouhania' is invoked by
the one making the prayer asking for protection against dangers that
might ensue through the intervention of Bintou.

cession—and struck the hawk with it three times. Then, as if quite satisfied with himself, he cried:

'Be off with you, you dirty bird! . . . Dirty thief!'

When the bird of prey had soared into the sky, I lowered my gaze: the chick, a little dazed, was hobbling toward his mother uttering little cries of fright and joy.

'My father!' I gasped. I couldn't think of another word to say . . .

'Yes,' he said. 'That is how, from time to time, we call our sons from a distance. Even those who live in Paris and who, like you, sometimes come bursting in upon us.'

He gave a smile. Marie was staggered. My mother, smiling too, seemed proud of her husband.

'And is that all you do?' I asked.

'Yes. Those words have a great deal of power. When one has spoken for the Lord, acted for the Lord, and lived alone in the wilderness for the Lord, as I have, in contemplation, and all for the Lord, then the Lord hearkens unto one when one prays to him.'

With a dismissive gesture, he stood up and walked toward the hut which was to be mine. I followed him. We followed him. And suddenly he said:

'If all these men and all these women, instead of wasting their days pronouncing childish discourses, were to consecrate that time to the adoration of the All-High, our native land would not be in its present wretched state. But now the All-High will punish them, for years and years, before allowing his pity and his blessing to descend upon them.'

'My father, did you say "blessing"'?

'Yes, his blessing upon this land which is being led astray. When the Black Lion comes, I shall no longer be here.'

'The Black Lion?' I asked.

'Yes, the heroic and infinitely wise Black Lion,

whom you know as well as I. Law and justice return also. And then ye shall be reconciled, reconciled with yourselves and with others. Yes, even with that country, that other country over there whose tongue you speak. I say unto you: if such be the will of Allah, blessed be thy name!'

'*Aminâ! Aminâ!*' I replied.

AFRICAN/AMERICAN LIBRARY
General Editor: Charles R. Larson

A continuing series of works of literary excellence by black writers
in the United States, Africa, and the Caribbean.